DAVY HARWOOD

TIJAN

Formatted by Elaine York / Allusion Graphics, LLC

Publishing & Book Formatting

www.allusiongraphics.com

DEDICATION

To my readers and those who have
continued to love Davy through the years.

PROLOGUE

I wasn't supernaturally inclined to know when vampires were around, but I knew anyway. I was empathic and that meant that I could feel what others felt, I felt what was going on around me. And right now, as I was on top of the Heffler where I volunteered for a crisis hotline, I knew there were eight nearby. I'd been the unfortunate one to answer the call and now I stood there, teetering on the edge with a 'jumper' before me. I was keenly aware of the two vamps behind me and the six on the ground. Vampires didn't usually care about death. I had no idea why they were there, but it didn't matter at that moment.

"Okay…okay." I took a deep breath and tried to inch forward.

The jumper was a frail looking girl with inflamed cheeks. Her red curls whisked around her from the wind, which didn't help our situation at all. She turned, saw me, and her eyes widened. She was the deer in my headlights, but I hoped that I wasn't the oncoming car to push her over the edge.

"Hi—hello—how are you? No—I mean…" I should have stopped then, but I was the only one from the hotline there. I'd been the last to leave and because of that, I was the only one that heard the phone, answered the phone, and figured out where the girl had called from.

I took another breath, and then said more calmly, "My name's Davina, but you can call me Davy—if you want." A part of me waited for the normal 'Stay away from me or I'll jump!', but it didn't come.

She didn't say a thing. I saw the tears and that's what made me pause. She'd been hysterical on the phone. I'd heard the words 'a guy', 'kill myself', and 'love.' My mind leapt to the natural clichéd conclusion. I thought she was going to kill herself over a guy and a part of me felt a little contempt for her. I know, I know — she's suicidal. I should be sympathetic, but… really—a guy?!

That had been my first reaction, but now I thought differently. This girl wasn't the suicidal virgin with a love gone reality. I looked into her hazel eyes and saw true agony in this girl. It was real and it blew my breath away for a moment. That was saying a lot.

"Okay." I needed to settle myself. I needed to plant both feet on the ground and I needed—I looked at her again. The pain was crippling. I could feel it. There was a sense of contentment and resolve in her too. This girl was done. What she was done with, I had no idea, but I felt it. She'd fought a battle, she'd lost, and she was done with it all.

For a moment, I stood in awe of her. I'd had my fair share of trauma and struggle, but I still had hope. This girl had none.

I closed my eyes and opened every sense I had. Every empath I knew would scream against this, but I needed to know what this girl had gone through. Something told me that I *needed* to know. I lowered my bridge, and I felt myself slip inside of her.

Turmoil. Desolation. Agony.

Worst of all, I felt the surrender. It slammed against me like waves of sleet in a downpour. It actually hurt and I bit my tongue. I wanted to feel more. I wanted to understand so I pushed further. Empaths are advised against this for a reason. If we touch too deep inside a person sometimes a part of us doesn't come back.

There was something inside of her, something that promised me that it'd be worth it. It was like… I needed to uncover it. Surging forward, I fought past the hopelessness and defeat. Then I reeled back when I touched the core.

There had been a guy. He had loved her. She had loved him… and then… I felt devastation, betrayal, and an end.

I gasped abruptly.

I don't know what happened, but something had happened. She had loved this guy. She found something and then… It was her decision, which was important. She decided when she'd die… not… I couldn't feel it anymore.

She gasped. My eyes flew open and I felt a wind propel me backwards. It was as if the universe didn't want me near this girl. I couldn't look away. Her eyes wanted to tell me something, something that she didn't even realize she wanted to say, but she didn't have the words or she didn't have the will. Then a single tear rolled down to join the rest and she smiled. It was haunting. Then she let go of the railing. I watched, stricken, but already in expectation as she soared downwards.

Something was off, something reeled inside of me.

Something had not gone according to plan and I'm the kind of girl where I knew that plans should go according to plan! It was usually highly essential, but this—this wasn't good. Not only for the fact that some part of me still felt connected to her, but there was a universe-world-future issue at stake. I had no idea why I felt that, how I felt it, but I did. I was panicked. The girl had jumped, and it was like the world was now going to end… I gulped.

CHAPTER ONE

"Mr. Moser is not happy."

That was my greeting as I dropped my books on the library table and plopped down next to my roommate. She was the originator of my stupid hotline volunteer career. The career that was *finito*, done, and over with. I snuck inside that morning, slipped the envelope underneath the door, and bolted.

There are occasions where I'm very much a coward, and this was one of those times.

"I'm not surprised," I muttered and bent to grab a pencil out of my bag. The location of the bag was just opportune. It was on the floor so I was able to turn and present my back to my roommate. I hoped she'd take the hint.

"What do you mean you're not surprised? Why aren't you surprised?" Emily hadn't taken the hint. Then again, she never did.

She had been my roommate for the last three months. Her entire life plan was written in detail with bulleted expenditure costs, but it all revolved around her career choice in social work. She was the one to volunteer at the hotline. She was the one who dragged me there. She was even the one that pointed out Adam. Emily wasn't the reason why I stayed. Adam was that reason.

I like boys. Most people would say that I'm boy-crazy, but the truth is I just find them entertaining. I would never ever kill myself over a guy. They're not worth that much, but they are worth a fun activity or a cuddle during a movie. When I saw his rich chestnut hair and almond eyes, I knew that Adam would make a great movie-cuddler.

"Davina!" Emily called out sharply. She was being ignored. That made her pissy.

I sighed and fought the urge to bury my head in my book. No. Why fight it? I buried my head into my book and groaned dramatically. I knew one thing. It would make Emily shut up. If there was one thing that made her uncomfortable, it was when someone was in need of emotional reassurance. I once saw her spill a drink and use that as an excuse to leave a group when one of the girls started crying. I highly doubted Emily's social work career would make it past the paper it was written on, but I wasn't going to be the one to tell her.

On another note, I hated being called Davina. It's Davy. It'll always be Davy. It'll never be Davina. Then I realized there was silence. Emily had quieted. I risked a look, and saw that her eyes were downcast on her own pile of books. I thanked my own quick wits for this reprieve.

"Davina."

I stiffened at the name, but when I looked over my shoulder I melted into a gooey feeling inside. Adam was approaching with an eager stride. His almond eyes sharpened with warmth, and I saw the earnest grin on his face. Tall, dark, and just pretty. That's how I'd describe my perfect guy, and Adam easily fit the bill. Plus, he wore Abercrombie. What girl didn't like that? Well, probably a lot, but it looked yummy on him.

"Hi, Adam." I was warm. I was always warm around him.

He stood at the end of our table and seemed riveted by me. I wondered why and then let it go. Obviously, the guy had woken up and realized his love for me.

"I heard about the suicide last night. Are you okay? You were there, right? That's what Shelly said."

Shelly. All the gooeyness dried up. Shelly was my competition. I cheated on my empath rules and took a peek inside her once. The feeling was mutual. She hated me even more and I didn't need to be psychic to know that she planned to murder me.

I was only joking…somewhat.

I was a short girl at five foot six inches with an average build, not slim, but not big either. I had brown curls on a good day, and a frizzy fray on a bad, but I knew my dark brown eyes and my full lips were my best features. Guys liked to stare at both of them, but Shelly was a tall willowy blonde with absolutely beautiful blue eyes. I always felt like I was swimming in a lake when I looked at them.

Shelly liked Adam. I liked Adam, but I wasn't sure who Adam liked.

"What else did Shelly say?" I couldn't hide my sarcasm.

Adam's smile dimmed slightly, but he pressed, "Is it true? You answered the phone and she was on the roof?"

The boy was goal oriented. "Yes. I was there, but she jumped."

Emily looked up with wide eyes. Adam shifted a little and his eyes skirted from me to Emily. "Are you… are you okay? Shelly said that you quit the hotline."

Emily harrumphed.

"Um…"

"I can't believe you quit." Emily had to put her two cents in.

"Yeah, I mean…" Adam took the seat next to mine and lowered his voice. It was soothing and seductive to my ears. "I mean…the place won't be the same without you, you know?"

Of course I knew, but that was the point of it. I wanted to get as far away as possible. It would always remind me of the girl from last night. I wasn't freaked out with agony and so forth, but the truth was that I was freaked out by the gut-wrenching feeling that something worldly awful had happened and that it was connected to me. "I just… it's too much, you know? I can't handle—she died in front of me. I can't…it's just too much for me."

I saw the sympathy in Adam. He placed his hand on mine. "I know exactly what you mean. If you ever need anything, call me. Okay? I want to help you through this tough time."

Emily fled the scene. I almost caught a back draft from her sprint. "I'd really like that, Adam."

He squeezed my hand. "Any time. Remember that, Davina."

I'd remind him another time not to call me that name.

Then the happily-ever-after feeling was gone as I felt a vampire walk past us. A cold wind slapped my insides and I looked up. Normally, vamps ignore me. They can't feel me like I can feel them so they just believe that they're not noticed.

Not this time.

I gasped when I saw a pair of coal-black eyes staring right back at me. The vamp was tall with jet black hair. He wore a white buttoned-down shirt over jeans. He kept going, but I still felt his eyes after he turned the corner.

"Davina," Adam said sharply, confused.

"What…what were you saying?" His hand was gone. I wanted his hand back.

"I…" He frowned again and asked, "Are you okay? You pushed me away and I mean, that's okay if that's what you need right now. I just thought…" He trailed off and looked away.

I didn't have to be empathic to see his insecurity. "It's not that. That guy scared me just now. I'm sorry. I want your help, I really do."

His eyes twinkled.

I sighed again. How could any girl not fall in love with how adorable he was?

"Can you two stop with the sappy moment?" Emily returned with a storm at her backside. She slumped in her seat. "I'm trying to study."

"Oh, yeah," Adam laughed, a little embarrassed. "I-uh—I'll talk to you later, Davina?"

I nodded. Hell yeah, we'd talk.

"Good. See you later then."

I glanced at Emily as he left and saw her sharp green eyes on me. She narrowed them in disgust.

"You make me sick."

"What? Why?" I was innocent.

"You totally lied to him just now. I had to run to the bathroom to keep from barfing. Really?! You can't handle it? She died in front of you? Mr. Moser told me that you need to get back to the hotline. You broke protocol and that's why you quit, not because you're 'emotionally shaken.' Seriously, Davina."

Maybe my roommate knew me a little better than I realized.

"Can you blame me?! Adam is to die for." I could not believe I just said those words.

"I can't believe you said that." Emily reiterated my thoughts.

I flushed, embarrassed, and leaned back in my chair. "What am I supposed to do? I didn't quit because of protocol, okay? And I need any advantage with Adam. You know Shelly Whistworth has her claws in him."

Emily was annoyed. "You have to go and talk to Mr. Moser. You did break the rules and he's worried about a lawsuit. And Adam Darley is not worth your time to lie and lower yourself. If he's a stand-up guy, he'll recognize that you're much more fun to be with than Shelly Witless. If he's not and he goes to her, he's not the guy that you'll want anyway."

"I'm not lowering myself," I remarked, and crossed my arms. "I'm just being manipulative."

Emily looked at me knowingly. "Well, stop. It's annoying."

"It's fun."

Emily opened her mouth and started to say something, but I felt the blast of cold race through me. My heart slowed as the vamp walked towards me from the opposite direction. His eyes were on me again. He seemed to look right through me, but he didn't slow his pace. He walked right past.

I hated vampires. I knew what they could do from personal experience. However, there were a lot of good vampires that liked to hang out on campus. Some of them even took classes and wanted to learn. This guy looked like a regular college student and he walked like one. Right to the computer lab, and back out again for a Mountain Dew. Typical college behavior, but I was betting he wasn't one of the 'good' vampires.

"Do you know who that is?"

"You interrupted me. I was talking."

I watched as he returned from the vending machines and sat back down at a computer. "That guy. Do you know him?"

"We're at a school with six thousand students. Really?! We're freshmen, Davina. How can you expect that I'd know him?"

I turned and regarded her. "Do you know him or not?"

She shifted uncomfortably in her seat.

"Who is he, Emily?" I leaned closer and hoped he couldn't hear us. There were two glass walls between us and the computer lab always buzzed with conversations and printing papers. If he tuned in, he could hear us, but for once I hoped that I wasn't a speck on this guy's radar. Correction—make that this vampire's radar.

"He's in my social work class."

"Intro?"

"Yeah. He's a junior and he's fulfilling a requirement." She sounded like she'd practiced that. Something felt off with her. She liked to share her opinions on people, but she didn't with this guy.

"You like him." I couldn't fault her. Vamps had seductive appeal down to perfection. Emily was a girl. Even *she* would fall under their power whether they intended it or not. The only way you could fight against their pull is if you knew what they were.

"I do not!" Emily cried out. She started to gather her books back up, but I laid a hand on them.

"It's okay. He's dreamy. I understand." I glanced back over, but sighed in disgust.

He just sat there at the computer. His hands didn't move on the keyboard. "Who is he?" I asked again, still watching the back of his head.

He sat rigidly.

"Luke Roane," Emily sighed. She'd be mortified at how dreamy it sounded.

"Roane?" I arched my eyebrows.

What kind of name was that? I'd heard of a Roane back home, but the name was only spoken about as a legend. Most of the vamps didn't believe he existed. I didn't like this new twist. My college life wasn't supposed to deal with supernatural things like this. I wanted an Adam in my life, not a vampire named Roane.

"He's really intelligent." Emily had opened her floodgates. Now her opinions flew freely. "He cares about the world and he's got some super insights into humanity."

I bet he did.

"Even Professor Sulls asks his opinions on matters. Luke's like no other guy that I know. I mean, I respect him. I have really high standards and I only respect two other guys," she said, casually.

"I know." I said dryly, "Jesus and Martin Luther King Jr."

"Can you believe it?" Emily sighed again. She was on the fast track for her first college lovecrush. It was my little name for those crushes when a girl thinks she's in love. They were annoying… to everybody.

Lovecrushes aside—or maybe front and center—I hadn't moved my eyes off Roane's back, but then my eyes slid past his shoulders to his black computer screen. I found myself staring smack head-on with him. I gasped in mortification. He'd been staring right at me the whole time. This was not good, not at all. He knew that I knew. I knew that he knew I knew. I could've pretended that I didn't know he was listening to us, but now all bets were off.

He'd seen.

I smiled smugly and whispered, "I know what you are."

His face didn't move. His eyes didn't react, but I knew I'd made him angry.

CHAPTER TWO

I called my empath sponsor and planned to meet her for coffee. When I pushed through the glass doors of Coffee Java, I inhaled the freshly brewed aroma and felt like I'd just touched a piece of heaven.

Blue looked up and waved an arm from a back booth tucked into the corner with bookcases and empty tables surrounding it. I liked how private it was. Blue got her name for her graying hair that she dyed with blue highlights. She liked that it gave her an out-of-this-world quality although she was very much an earthly woman. Every one of the bracelets jangling on her wrist stood for a cause – pollution, cancer, save the forests, happiness from an orgasm.

I smiled widely as I weaved my way through the book cases. "Blue-cheese, how are you?"

She laughed with her raspy deep-throated voice. "That never gets old." Nudging forward a coffee, she added, "Take it. You know it's for you."

I nabbed it and closed my eyes when the liquid touched my lips. It was so good, so yummy, and I knew I really *was* in heaven.

She closed the novel she'd been reading and pushed it to the side. She wasn't one for idle talk. "Okay, girl. Out with it."

"I have a problem."

She arched a perfectly outlined eyebrow and rested her chin on her hand.

"I have *vamp* problems," I said further.

Understanding dawned in her grey eyes. All empaths understood that statement. Sometimes we felt too much, but when we felt a vampire our senses went haywire from what *they* felt. "Are you still practicing your blocks?"

I nodded. I'd upped my level since I joined the hotline.

"That's good. Keep at it. Now, tell me about the vamp problem."

What could I say? "It's nothing really, but a feeling. He saw me in the library today with my roommate. I asked her about him and he heard the whole thing."

Blue frowned. Her purple lips rubbed together. "What's the problem? Vamps are used to that."

"I was watching him when I asked her about him. I didn't realize that he'd been watching the entire time."

"What do you mean 'watching'?" She narrowed her eyes.

"He knew that I knew what he was. It was like a challenge or something. I didn't like it."

"Oh, girl." Blue frowned deeply this time. "What'd you do?"

I took a sip of my coffee, but the flavor didn't taste heavenly anymore.

"Girl."

"I might've said something like 'I know what you are' …or something."

She pursed those purple lips together and reached for her coffee. I felt her disapproval coming at me in waves. "You did what?"

"I couldn't help it, alright? It was like he was challenging me or something."

Blue sat her coffee down and leaned forward in a matronly way. "You know better, Davina. You have issues with vampires. We all do, but you've got more. You gotta fight that. Now what's gonna happen? You know vampires. They love challenges. He's going to be all over you now. *Then* what? How are you going to get away?"

In a small voice, I murmured, "I could always do what I did before."

Blue let out a disgusted sound and rolled her eyes. "I would not recommend lighting a vampire on fire. It didn't help you back home. It won't help you this time. Learn from your mistakes, child."

My back stiffened at that. I hated being called Davina and I *really* hated being called 'child'. "You know, maybe moving here and having you so close isn't all that great."

"I'm being your sponsor. You know the steps. If you've got vamp problems, you've done step one. You've told me. Good job, but you need to be held accountable for the next step. Which is?"

She knew I knew it, but I cringed when I had to say it. "I have to attend an empath meeting."

"And?"

"And...," This was so freaking hard. "...I have to tell the group."

"About?"

I growled deep in my throat. "I have to tell them about Craig and how I lit him on fire because he was stalking me."

Pride gleamed from Blue and she smiled blindingly. "That's my girl. You know the deal. Vampires have their twisted thing for us. The good ones avoid us out of respect and the bad ones—you know more than most."

I swallowed tightly. Craig had reveled in my torment. He'd become obsessed with me. He stalked me and he loved that I couldn't block him. Vampires were overpowering, much more so than humans. An empath could easily block humans at a level four, but it wasn't until level six that we could easily block vampires. Craig met me when I was on level five. Luckily, the night that I'd snapped and lit him on fire was the night that I broke to level six. I remembered that night. I saw him on fire and I remembered the pain that engulfed him while I stood back to watch.

"Girl." Blue's calming voice brought me back. She had opened herself up and I could feel some of the pain taken from me.

"Don't do that," I murmured huskily. I didn't want her to feel my pain. No one should be burdened with that.

She reached over and placed a hand on mine. It instantly calmed me and I turned my palm upwards to link our fingers. Blue smiled gently. "There's a reason why we're empaths, Davy. You know that. I like to help a little bit, every now and then."

'Every now and then' was the empath community's motto. We all learned that we could help every now and then, but not too much to kill ourselves. Too many had died because they tried to help too much.

"Now," Blue squeezed my hand. "What are you going to do with your current vampire?"

"Oh…" I took a deep breath. "I don't know. I'll have to see what kind of vampire he is. He might be one of the good ones."

Blue twisted her lips in disbelief.

"I mean, he seems to be one of the student vampires." The chances were fifty-fifty. The bad ones pretended to be college students to hunt.

"There's a meeting next week. You should go."

I'd have to go — it'd be good for me.

"So, tell me about your crazy uptight roommate." Blue's eyes rekindled with gentleness. She knew I needed a lighter topic. The 'Craig topic' was deep enough for me. So I sat back and entertained her with Emily stories. By the end of our meeting, I hadn't said a word about the suicidal girl. I knew I should have, but I was still uneasy thinking about it. Some things were too hard or too scary to put into words.

When I returned to campus that evening, I faltered as I got out of my car. The air was chilled, but there was something else, something supernatural in it. Looking over my shoulder I only saw a parking lot full of cars. There was a clump of trees at the north end of the lot, but I'd go south to my dorm. I held my breath as I walked underneath two tall oaks and an arched overhang that led into the quad of my dorm.

Throwing my bag over my shoulder, I marched forward. No shadows moved and none seemed to watch me in return. I breathed easier when I neared the main doors. Once inside, excited voices came from the television room.

We were allowed boy visitors, but a lot of girls used the lounges for their study groups. It wasn't unusual to look inside to see books and papers sprawled across the beige carpeting right alongside sleeping students. This is what I saw as I peeked inside, but I wasn't ready for the sight of my roommate in a corner chair with a wistful smile on her face. She glowed.

I was floored. There was no Roane. There was no professor. There were no school books and yet, Emily glowed. Her straight blonde hair fell freely over her shoulders and she even had a tint of lip gloss on.

Had we all gone to hell and I missed the bus?

Then I felt the cold flare inside again. I felt him behind me before I looked, but when I did I found myself staring into the blackest coal eyes that I'd ever seen. Craig had looked at me with those same eyes the night he died. I shivered at the memory.

Luke Roane saw the tremor. His eyes raked me up and down and it was like we were caught in a heated debate, but there were no words. It wasn't my first vampire face-off, but this was different than the others.

I should've been able to easily block this vamp, but I felt the curtain slowly lift and I couldn't do anything about it. I always felt their cold, but usually it was just a tickle. This time I felt the full blast of his darkness. It worked its way up my feet to my legs, past my knees, and over my waist. I fought it off, but it kept coming. The evil started to wrap itself around me. I felt its tentacles grasp my arms and start to squeeze me tight.

All the while, he watched me with no emotion.

Not me. I couldn't hide my struggle. My teeth started chattering. When I felt the first poke in my chest, I shoved past him and hurried to my room. After I burst through the door to my room, the spell lessened immediately, but I was panting to catch my breath.

I heard my phone start to ring and knew it was Blue. She'd be the first to feel my panic. At that moment, I hated the lack of privacy with empaths.

I ignored the phone and slid down the door to breathe in and out.

I'd felt evil before. I'd felt it from Craig many times, but not to this extent. I'd never felt like it wanted to squeeze the life out of me, have it wrapped around my heart. It felt like it wanted my soul.

I shuddered again. I needed warmth. I needed a distraction. Hell, I could use this to my advantage.

I pulled out my phone and dialed Adam's number since I'd programmed it in the first day when we'd gotten the Hotline Volunteer Directory.

Adam picked up on the second ring. "Hello?"

I purposely didn't fight the slight tremor in my voice. "Adam?"

"Davina? Are you okay?"

"Yeah, yeah, I mean—I think—"

"What's wrong? Did something happen? Do you need to talk?"

"I…" I sighed to myself. I needed to be honest. It was Blue's motto. I was about to use this boy, but I liked him. He was normal. He was human. My hands tightened around the phone. "Can you come over?"

His answer was swift. "I'll be there in ten minutes."

"Thanks, Adam." I hung up and fell back against the door. And the strange thing, I really was thankful.

When I heard a knock at the door, I screamed and shot to my feet. I knew who was on the other side, although I couldn't feel him. "Go away." I flinched when I heard my voice. It was raw and vulnerable. *I* was raw and vulnerable.

He knocked again, but slower this time. I snorted. Really?! Did he think it would be more dramatic that way?

"Go away!" I yelled this time. I wasn't scared of vamps. I was just scared of *this* vamp. The door seemed large and luminous. I watched as it seemed to grow before me. It was like it was just waiting for me to answer it.

I don't know how long I stood there.

"Davina? It's me." I jumped when I heard another abrupt knock, but relaxed instantly. It was Adam. A whole host of relief, warm fuzzies, and other feelings rushed through me at the sound of his voice. Nice and normal.

Flinging open the door, I launched myself at him. He even smelled normal. If I knew I wouldn't scare him away, I would've wrapped my legs around his waist. "I am so glad you're here," I jumbled out with my nose pressed into his masculine-smelling sweater.

Adam laughed, caught off guard, and held me up. "I'm glad that you're glad."

Right. Human. I needed to act human. I unglued myself and pulled back. "Sorry. I…uh…sorry. I'm just…" I felt stupid.

"Emotional," Adam offered.

He was awesome.

"That's okay. Mr. Moser said it's good to let yourself feel. Let it flow naturally, Davina. Really. That's the only way you can start healing." Adam enfolded me tighter and tucked his chin in the crook of my neck. "Let it out, Davina. Let it out."

His blue sweater felt warm against my skin. He smelled of pine trees and musk. I inhaled deeper and smelled a little vanilla in there too. This is what it would be like if we were boyfriend and girlfriend. I might need him. He'd come to hug me and the world would melt away.

"Ahem."

We turned to see Emily glaring at us with her arms crossed and annoyed.

"What?" I was having a moment.

She rolled her eyes. "You have a visitor downstairs."

"Who?"

Emily shrugged impatiently and pushed past us to her closet. She flung open the door and grabbed a brush. As she combed her hair and reached for some lipstick, she remarked, "Some girl who looks like a stripper."

That could have been anyone according to Emily's standards. "She didn't give a name?"

"What am I–your receptionist?" Emily gave me a disgusted look, slammed her closet door shut, and stormed past me. Adam whistled underneath his breath.

I didn't know why Emily was so pissed, and at that moment I didn't care. She'd go back down, make crooning noises with the vampire, and be her oddly gushing self in a moment. I had three things on my mind: visitor, vampire, and Adam.

"I guess the news got out, huh?" Adam stuffed his hands into his front pockets, which made him look leaner and taller. The soft shadow from our poorly lit dorm room seemed to soften his features and his blue eyes looked adorable. My tongue might've just fallen out.

Then I heard what he said. "Wait. What news?"

"The girl that jumped – it's all over the news."

That didn't bode well with me. "Uh…" I ran a hand through my hair and cringed. My hair must've looked like a bird's nest.

"You look fine," Adam reassured me.

"Thanks." I still turned and found a mirror. Not bad. My normally frizzy hair actually looked shiny and healthy. Wonders never ceased.

"So I guess…your visitor, huh?"

"Want to walk down with me? Make sure it's not someone creepy?"

Adam looked relieved and concerned at the same time. I chose to think he was concerned for my benefit. When we reached the stairway, I was surprised when I felt Adam grab my hand. He looked embarrassed. "Just in case it's someone you don't want around."

"You're going to play my protective boyfriend?" I teased.

His cheeks turned pink. Adorable. I squeezed his hand and said in all honesty,

"Thanks, Adam. It means a lot."

When we moved through the bottom doorway, I stopped dead in my tracks. My focus zoomed in on the petite blonde who had wrapped herself around Emily's vampire. One of her leather clad legs rubbed up and down against his calf and her cleavage was barely hidden underneath a tight black lace tank top poised perfectly for his viewing pleasure. Her crystal blue eyes snapped up and latched onto mine.

I knew why Emily was so furious.

Kates Heath, a childhood *nostalge*— another one of my words that I used to describe childhood friends that you remained friends with because of nostalgic memories and nothing else — was the epitome of every man and boy's fantasy of a bad girl. Vampires ate girls like her for breakfast or they would if they could.

"Heya, celebrity," Kates drawled in her husky voice and whipped her dusky blonde hair around.

"Kates." I refused to look the vampire in the eyes.

Slowly, with hypnotizing grace, Kates unwrapped herself from him and stood to cross the room towards me. I felt the tension in the air. The entire room had been watching and now everyone held their breaths at our next move.

I flicked my gaze to Emily. She looked like a bomb ready to explode so I latched onto Kates' arm and yanked her behind me. Dragging her outside, we circled around the corner and through an alcove of trees in the far corner before I whirled and snapped, "What are you doing here?"

Kates looked taken aback, but her smoky laugh rang out. "I can't believe you. Look at you. You're all…College Barbie."

"What are you doing here, Kates? You're not supposed to be here."

Kates chuckled. "You're too much sometimes, Davy. Get over it. You know exactly why I'm here."

"No. I don't."

She groaned and placed her hands on her hips. "Steven saw you on the news. He called me and I headed here. You're on the freaking news, Davy. You know how bad that is…for you."

"Nine o'clock news. That was a half hour ago. There is no way that you drove from home in thirty minutes." We lived five hours away.

"It was on the five o'clock news, Barbie Doll."

Did it even matter? "You can't be here," I hissed.

Kates smiled smugly and shifted comfortably back on her heels. "You've got me, whether you want me or not. Who's the hottie vampire, by the way? He's delicious."

I grimaced, but warned, "Stay away from him."

"Why?"

"What do you mean 'why'? He's a vampire."

Kates shrugged. "He's hot. I caught a peek at his marking. He's a Hunter."

"Kates." I shook my head, and sighed. Nothing was going how it was supposed to… I didn't even know what to think about him being a Hunter.

"What?" Kates piped up, dumbfounded. "Look. I'm just here to watch your back. When I think you're covered, I'll head out. Promise."

"I don't need this. I can't… "

"You were on the news. They talked about that suicidal girl and that someone from the hotline was there. They didn't say your name, but it won't matter. They're going to get calls from people wanting their five minutes of fame. It's only a matter of time before you're hunted down. Let's hope that no one finds out about your special gifts."

Kates was right. Things were going to get bad, really bad. Here I was, concerned about Emily's vampire and Shelly Witless. This reminded me— "Adam is mine."

"Ooh—who's Adam?"

"None of your business." I was adamant.

"It might become my business. I'm bunking with you until it all blows over."

Oh no.

CHAPTER THREE

The next morning, I opened my eyes and instantly groaned. When Kates and I had returned to the dorm last night, I'd been ecstatic to find the vampire gone, but disappointed to find Adam gone too However, Emily *had not* been happy to meet our newest roommate. Kates ate it up. She loved causing drama and I could see that Emily was her newest target.

I woke Kates up and made her promise to play nice, which she did with a gleam in her eyes.

Later, when I let myself in my dorm room, I knew Kates had found a loophole. Emily jumped on me and crowded me against the door. "She has to go! Now."

"What? I don't—" Although, I could guess.

Emily shot up a hand. "Or I'm calling the cops on her."

Sadly, I wasn't surprised. This was just how Kates got her jollies. "What'd she do?"

"What'd she do? What didn't she do?!" Emily laughed in outrage. She crossed her arms and I almost saw a cloud of smoke puff out of her ears.

Kates sauntered in with a towel and a thong dangling from her hand. A coy smile was outlined by ruby red lips. "Heya, you're back."

I moved Emily aside and hung up my bag. "I'm tired. I'm hungry. And," I looked at Emily. "I'll deal with Kates later."

A look of disgust flashed over her face before she harrumphed once and left.

"So... how many vamps did you see? I've seen fourteen and I haven't left this building."

"Uh huh." When I sat down, I didn't want to deal with vamps, my roommate, or my nostalge.

Kates dropped into Emily's chair beside me. "I want to know what's going on with the vampire population. I've been to colleges before. I've been to *this* college before and I remember seeing four, not fourteen."

"So what?" I sighed as I glanced at the message machine. Twenty-three messages. Apparently, the word got out that I'd been on that roof. "What am I supposed to do?"

Kates threw a toned leg on the desk. "It's weird that you're famous. I would love to be famous, but not you. We all know your deal—"

"Emily doesn't," I intervened quickly.

"Really? She doesn't know? No wonder she's pissy at me. I know something she doesn't and she knows it. Anyways, let's hope the reporters don't find out you think of yourself as an empath."

"I am."

"They won't think that." She waved it off. "They'll paint you as some psycho and you'll be blamed for that girl jumping. So the question is how long can you avoid them? Or is that going to make them hungrier?"

Everyone in the psychic community had grown up with strict guidelines on how to handle possible exposure. Some followed and some didn't. The ones that the media reported on, they either didn't care or they wanted their moment of fame. I could handle the media.

"Why so many vampires?" I wondered out loud instead. I didn't want to discuss my current celebrity status.

Kates shrugged and stood up. She dropped the towel and bent over to look through my closet. I was relieved to see that she wasn't naked. "I know you're all demure when you're around me, but you have some rocking clothes. Like this one!" She produced a pair of black leather pants.

"That's for a Halloween costume." Not really. They were for Adam... the when and where was still up to debate.

Kates snorted and slipped the pants on. She chose a near-see-through cream colored shirt. "I think we should go and 'interview' that hottie from last night."

"No, we won't."

Kates heard the emotion and whipped around. Her crystal blue eyes pierced straight through me. "Out with it. Now."

"I don't like him. That's all you need to know."

"Right, because the last time you slammed this wall between us things were just *peachy* then too."

I glowered. "There was a reason I wasn't feeling so friendly towards you. You were dating the guy that I was daydreaming about. I'd be stupid to have trusted you back then."

She flipped her blonde hair over her shoulder. "I only dated him because that bitch told me you were into Chris. I thought *you* were the backstabbing whore." That bitch would never be named. She'd driven a wedge between two best friends and she'd paid for her crimes, but we were still bitter.

I stood slowly. "We both know that I wasn't into Chris."

"I know... now."

"Yes... you do."

Kates snorted in disgust. "I really hate her for what she did."

Warily, I looked at the blinking voice messages. "Food? Or drink?"

Kates snorted again. "Do you have to ask?"

Kates and I always had fun on our night outs. Sometimes that was the only time we had fun. A flood of memories rushed through me and I turned to snatch my fake license. For that night I'd be Silvia Dellawoy, a ripe twenty-two year old from Hillsfield, Illinois. I just hoped that I wouldn't meet a bouncer from Hillsfield, Illinois. "Let's go, Tammy."

Kates laughed huskily as she reached for the door. "Oh honey.

You might not like that vampire, but I know a place where the werewolves hang out. You'll love them."

Did Kates know me or what? I loved werewolves. They worked so hard at suppressing their own urges I didn't have to block them. They blocked themselves.

"But you're changing clothes," Kate announced and scoured my closet to pull out a pair of blue jean tights with a sparkly low cut v-neck top. I eyed the clothes, but knew it was a lost battle. Kates always had her way and it had been a long time since I'd let my hair down, not literally though.

When we left the dorm, I made sure we took the back stairway. It was easier and no one needed to stare from the front television lounge, no one that we wanted. Kates reached for the exit door, but paused when the bottom door opened. I heard a familiar tap of heels on the stairs and cringed. That's when Emily rounded the stairs and blinked in surprise at the sight of us. She carried a steaming bowl of oatmeal in her hands. I saw her stiffen.

We were dressed for a nightclub, a top notch nightclub, and Emily was dressed for oatmeal. She wore a pair of flannel pajama pants with a baggy sweatshirt and rabbit slippers. The white ears drooped over and touched the floor.

"We're… uh…"

"We're going out." Kates smiled and looped her elbow through mine.

I felt like we were the popular beautiful girls as we stared down one of the unpopular, dowdy girls. I hated it.

Removing my elbow, I smiled nervously. "You want to come with us?" I didn't want to be one of those girls. I liked oatmeal too. Kates gasped. Emily was floored. I insisted, "You must. Kates will even do your hair!"

Kates snorted abruptly.

"Okay…" Emily didn't sound too sure.

As all three of us slowly traipsed back to the room, I only hoped that Emily wouldn't realize we were going to a werewolf bar. If she did… holy crap.

When we got out of the car, much later, outside the local werewolf bar, I glanced at Emily as she smoothed her pressed shirt down and nervously checked the rest of her clothes. She looked uncomfortable. Kates had wound Emily's hair into a braid that wove around her head. With the make-up job Kates provided, Emily looked a little hip hop, but she held strong with the clothes. We wanted her to wear a pair of tattered tight blue jeans and a loose-fitting pink and silver tank top, but Emily was adamant. She wore khaki pants with a buttoned-down pressed pink shirt. She looked like a librarian with costume make-up.

She would stick out like blood to sharks. Luckily, we weren't going to a vampire bar. They would've been all over her. Werewolves stuck to their own kind and they looked human. It was only when their fur started to grow that a human would freak out. I hoped our night would not end with a freaking Emily.

"Okay. Let's go!" Kates yanked me forward. Emily followed at a sedate pace, but when I looked over my shoulder I saw she was biting her lip. She was warily eyeing the bar's sign and I felt her nervousness. It pounded me like hail.

Once inside, Kates dragged us to get drinks, but Emily hung back. Three shots were ordered and when Kates tried to give one to Emily, it was declined. Then I saw the evil delight turn my way. She pushed the shot at me and I downed two right away. I wasn't even going to fight Kates. I needed to save my energy for Emily. Someone would have to make sure she didn't end up dead. Not Kates, she laughed in delight and turned to order another four shots.

We were in for a rough night.

Then I looked over Emily's shoulder and gulped when I saw a muscular guy with blonde dreadlocks lick his lips as he eyed Emily's backside. Blood to sharks. He nudged his buddy and both of them turned to lap her up. Then their eyes slid to mine and I sucked in my breath horrified. We weren't at a werewolf bar. Bud's was a vampire bar.

I grabbed Kates.

"Hey! Watch the beer!" I saw the brimming pitcher and felt the cool liquid splash on my arm, but I was infuriated. I could give a damn about beer and I don't normally think blasphemous thoughts like that.

Beer was holy.

"I have to talk to you. Alone."

Kates saw my fury. I realized that she'd known the whole time.

"What's going on?" Emily spoke up.

"Nothing. I just… I have to go to the bathroom."

"Oh. I have to go too," Emily gushed out, relieved.

"No!" I barked. I saw that Emily was taken aback so I gentled my tone, "I meant… alone."

"Oh. Okay."

"We'll be back," I hurried out and yanked Kates behind me.

"But… alone…?"

Storming off and dragging Kates with me, I roughly pushed our way through the crowd. I felt each of them when my arms or shoulders made contact, but I just gritted my teeth against the pain. Vampires felt too much hatred for me. I should've been able to automatically block them, but I was angry. Plus, I hadn't been prepared.

An entire bar of vampires was not my night of fun.

When I pushed into the bathroom, I saw two vamp girls at the mirror. "Get out! Now."

They turned, annoyed, and stopped short. One of them gasped, but the other looked like she was going to argue before the other dragged her outside. I knew that I should've cared about what I'd just seen since vamps don't follow orders unless there was a reason, but I didn't.

Flipping the lock, I rounded on Kates. "How could you?!"

She rolled her eyes and approached the mirror. As she primped her hair, she shrugged. "You have to get over this hang-up with vamps, Davy."

"Hey," I pointed a finger at her. "You should have just as much of a hang-up with them. I mean—"

Kates rounded and stared at me. I saw the warning, but I didn't heed it. "Your mother used to kill vampires. We all know what they did to her."

"You don't talk about that. Ever!" Kates seethed.

"They branded you—"

"Shut up!"

"I know your mom was a slayer, but they slaughtered her, Kates. How can you be okay coming here?"

Kates slapped me. I fell against the wall and tasted blood on the inside of my cheek, but I rounded back and exclaimed, "You had no right bringing me here. You *really* had no right bringing Emily."

Oh god. I gulped. Emily had been left alone. Throwing open the door, I hurled myself through the crowd. I know that I jarred a bunch of them, but I didn't care. I just needed to find my roommate and get out of there. We were like sitting ducks in Dodge.

Then I stopped in my tracks and my mouth fell to the floor. Emily sat, squashed in a booth, with three vampires around her and at the end sat her Luke Roane vampire. He looked relaxed, lounging back in the booth, but I saw the way his eyes darted over his men and Emily. He didn't share in the conversation, but he was in control of it. They glanced at him occasionally, like they were waiting for a signal from him to change the subject.

He didn't. He looked content and yet, he still looked like the predator he was even though he dressed like a normal college student with tight-fitting shirts and trendy blue jeans. He wore a black shirt that molded to his lean form.

I could tell Emily was miffed that she didn't sit beside him, but she was still all smiles. Vomit came up in the back of my throat, but I swallowed it back down. He didn't deserve her gushy fuzzies.

"That's why I brought you here." Kates paused behind me. "He's a Hunter, Davy. You know what they do. You want to know why all those vampires are on campus, ask him."

I watched how the vampires instinctually felt Kates' approach. They all looked up with eager eyes, but not him. He turned and looked straight at me. I met his gaze without a flinch, even though I felt my insides snap. I had to hold it in, he couldn't know. Then I glanced to his collarbone where a corner of his shirt had fallen to the side and saw the beginning of his mark.

I didn't need to see all of it because I'd seen it before. It was the mark that all Hunters were branded with once they'd gotten their first kill. It was a symbol of interlocking crosses with the Hebrew inscription for remembrance in the middle. Craig told me once that the symbol stood for their humanity. They were branded to remember what it was like to be human, so they could keep a reverence for the humans that they'd sworn to protect. The Hunters were an elite league and a vampire had to be invited by the Elders. Only a handful roamed and guarded each state.

As I watched Emily's smile slip at Kates' arrival, I knew that they were both safe. Hunters guarded against the Craigs of the vampire world. They hunted their own, the ones that refused to accept the new decree not to harm humans. Two Hunters had arrived and ripped Craig to shreds with no jury or bargain when I'd lit him on fire. They were judges in themselves and those two Hunters had made their judgment on Craig.

Suddenly feeling nauseous, I pushed through the crowd to a side door and found myself in a back alley.

The door hadn't closed behind me before I heard him. "You're running away."

He leaned against the door, relaxed and primed for attack. His fangs didn't show, but I wondered if he'd had them ready for me. Something told me this vampire wouldn't mind violating his decree with me.

"You're using my friend." I thought I caught a flash of amusement, but it disappeared just as quick.

He remarked, emotionless, "They're using me."

Kates was. Emily wasn't.

'You're not good with your own shield.' I heard him in my mind and gasped before I shoved him out. I was more irritated he'd gotten in without me realizing because I was better than that. He smiled and I bared my teeth. "You don't get to read my mind."

"Not anymore. You just blocked me," he spoke, bored, and had the nerve to stretch in front of me.

"You're an asshole." He was getting harder to block, not from my mind but from feeling him. Though, it wasn't like the last time. I didn't feel the evil reach inside of me.

He laughed, but his eyes were so cold. "You've never spoken to me and this is our first exchange? Oh wait, you taunted me, right? 'I know what you are.' Isn't that what you said or did I get it wrong? You think I'm some animal."

I lashed out, "Been taking trips in my mind?"

"I haven't needed to," he shot back. His eyes sparked a bit. "You read loud and clear. I'm surprised you've gotten away with it for so long."

I frowned. "What are you talking about?"

"Lying. All you do is lie. I've known about you for a couple of days, but I could tell right away."

"I don't lie." I reacted, tersely, and my hands formed tight fists.

He looked down at them, but he smirked. "Yes, you do. That's all you do. You lie to that boy you've got dancing to your tune. You lie to your roommate. She doesn't know who we are. You're lying to yourself when you think you don't want Kates here."

I stiffened at his proclamations. He had no idea… "Get away from me and stay away from my friends."

Something went flat in his eyes. The look had been there, but I hadn't seen it till it was gone. It vanished completely now and I knew he was furious. "Your friends won't stay away from me."

"How do you know Kates?" I asked. He'd mentioned her by name, which meant something. I remembered the two vampire females in the bathroom. They'd either known me or they'd known Kates. I needed to know why…

I suddenly felt sick. I felt actual vomit surge up in my throat, but I clamped a hand over my mouth and whirled to a corner. It spewed out before I could stop it. He was quiet behind me. I expected some taunting, but there were none.

"What?" I asked weakly as I wiped at my mouth. "No words to insult me with? Maybe I'm just drunk."

"You could be. You drank what? Four shots?"

So he'd been watching from the beginning…

"I highly doubt it." Something was off in his tone, like he knew something that I didn't. I wasn't pleased with it. I felt that he wasn't pleased either. That's when I gasped further and wretched again.

I had been feeling him. Somehow, I'd slipped inside without the evil lashing at me. As I glanced at him through watery eyes, I saw that his mind was elsewhere. He didn't know I felt inside of him. I took a small breath and stilled, concentrating to explore what else was in him. Duty. It blared at me. I was startled by that, but then I surged further and tentatively touched what was beneath it, pain. It was blistering. It reminded me of the girl on the roof. She'd felt the same pain, but unlike her surrender this vampire was firmly and completely devoted to… something. He defied death or maybe death retreated from him. I'd never felt what I felt from him.

"Stop that!" He hurled me out of him.

I gasped and fell against the bricked wall. My arm scraped against the roughness and I watched, frozen, as his coal eyes took on a keen alarmed look. The air was charged around him. I sucked in a breath and smelled what he did. My skin had torn from the wall and even I could smell the blood in the alley.

"Are you an animal?" I whispered my challenge and waited for his response. It was like something inside of me had uttered those words, something that wasn't from me—and he knew it.

He blocked me. I shielded him. And yet—there was something else, some entity, that felt the other between us. Suddenly, it was too much and I gutted out, "Get away from me!" The connection was destroyed and I felt it reel inside of me.

"Gladly." Acid dripped from him and he was gone in the next second.

The door slammed behind him and I was left to gasp for breath at his abrupt exit. It was too much. His presence had been too much. Too many things swirled around inside of me, but I closed my eyes and concentrated on breathing. I remained there until I felt my feet beneath me, until I was able to stand and breathe at the same moment.

Then I remembered my question. He'd known about Kates, but I didn't know how. I needed to know for her safety.

CHAPTER FOUR

I went back inside, but the moment I approached their booth Roane jerked his head towards the door. The other vampires stood and followed him. Kates frowned at the abrupt exit, but Emily gushed with a glazed look over her face.

She smiled at me with stars in her eyes. "Did you see him, Davy?"

I had more than seen him, but I wasn't about to share that with her. I asked Kates, "What happened to her? She looks drunk." There were no empty glasses in front of Emily.

"What do you think?"

Kates was still annoyed with me, but my stomach rumbled and I pressed a hand over it. I had worse things on my mind. With a closer look at Emily, I saw the glazed eyes, flushed lips, pink cheeks, and then I saw her neck. There was a small red mark over her artery. "What did they do?"

"What do you think?" Kates asked flatly, bored. Hell, she probably watched the whole time.

Vampires weren't supposed to feed off humans, but I knew a few of them used lovebites to sneak a taste. It was frowned upon by the Elders, but not strictly prohibited—especially when it happened in a bar. It was considered the same as making out to them.

"I'm bored," Kates announced.

Emily smiled, drunkenly. "Did you see him, Daveeena? He was here and then he was… out there and now… he's… he went that way." She swung her hand towards the door and smiled sleepily.

"Maybe we should go."

Emily protested, "But… he's…"

"Not coming back, wino." Kates snorted and stood. She stretched and pretended to heave a big yawn—her boobs arched in the air.

I rolled my eyes. "Come on, Emily. I'll get you home."

Kates dropped her arms abruptly. "You had four shots. You can't drive anywhere."

"I'm fine. Really." I could've told her about the nausea, but she was mad. I wasn't feeling all friendly and soul-confessing.

"Well…" Kates raked us up and down and then glanced over her shoulder. "I think I might stay. I'll give you a call."

Emily stumbled, but I caught her. Then I frowned even more when I saw her cheeks pale abruptly. Lovebites are just that—they're little nips. They don't take too much blood, but she was reacting as if they drank her empty.

"Did you drink?" It would explain a little…

"She had some beer. She'll be fine. Take her home, get her in bed. She'll be the same tomorrow."

I didn't bother to ask Kates how she'd get back. I knew she'd be fine or sleep somewhere else. She was still branded and a lot of vampires held a grudge. "Just… be safe."

"Yeah. Whatever."

"Seriously, Kates. Safe, not stupid, remember?"

"Yeah. I know," she grumbled and shoved through the crowd. I watched as she disappeared into the bathroom until Emily stumbled in the opposite direction. Someone caught her and pushed her ahead. I tried to grab her, but someone else bumped her further ahead. Pretty soon, I watched helplessly as Emily managed to fall out the front door backwards.

Talk about exits.

I darted through the crowd and found Emily on the wet sidewalk, ashen, and with mud on her khakis. If the girl could see herself, she'd be mortified. She looked like every other drunkard.

"Come on. Let's go."

I bent forward to help her stand. Fishing the keys out of her pocket, I guided her to the car and in the backseat. My inner empath alarm was going off when we drove off. There were an inappropriate number of vampires. My home town had a population of 2,000. Southdale wasn't big, but it wasn't a three hundred bump in the road. We averaged five or six vamps. Benshire was at least 12,000. That meant there should be around 200 hundred vamps around. I knew the vampire population would be significantly more compared to home, but as I drove past Bud's, I saw more than I should've trolling the streets and alleys.

Emily puffed out a snore and there was a speck of drool at the corner of her mouth. Of course. She'd be one of those slobbering drunks when she drank. Then I remembered the red mark. The vampire drank from her. That meant some of him was in her. It was a small bit, but it was something. My stomach rolled over on itself as I considered the possibilities.

Too many vampires. That girl had jumped from my building and eight vamps had been there. A Hunter was here and he looked like he was permanently staying. Something was going on.

No—forget it! I did not want to get involved with the local vampire political crap. They had their own community. As long as they stayed away from me…, but they hadn't stayed away from Emily. I was worried they wouldn't stay away from Kates. She'd been branded as a slayer's daughter. It was known that a vampire slayer's strength passes to her daughter at the slayer's death. The vamps hadn't hurt Kates then, but if they saw the burned mark in her skin they'd know that Kates had the strength of a slayer. She could handle her own, I knew that, but I knew that a lot of them still held resentment towards slayers of all kinds—the good and bad. If there was an overabundance of vampires in the area, which I was pretty sure there was, chances were good that some of those with chips on their fangs would be in town. If they ran into Kates… who knew what would happen.

I had to know. It was for Kates' safety.

Suddenly, I felt like I would vomit again. I pressed my arm over my stomach, but it didn't help. I felt the first gag and veered the car over to the edge. Bursting through the door, I upchucked my entire stomach contents on the side of the road. When I leaned back on my knees, I warily eyed three vamps in the alley. I waited, since I didn't know what they would do. If it came to it, I could probably obliterate a vampire just from my breath. It was rank.

"Davy?"

"Yeah?" I wiped my mouth and moved back to the seat.

Emily peered at me through foggy eyes, haphazard hair, and pasty white cheeks. Talking about vampires…

"Where'd you go?" She frowned, confused.

I held the steering wheel in my hands, but I needed a breath to settle my stomach. "Nowhere. You fell asleep."

She giggled. "Did you see him? He was there. He didn't talk to me, not really, but he was there. Am I pathetic? I think I need to do something. Maybe I could—what kind of girls do you think he likes? I bet he likes girls like your friend. She's a little skanky, sorry. I'm not able to stop what I'm saying before I say it. But she is."

"Don't worry, Ems. I know what you think about Kates, but… there's more to her. Trust me. She's a good friend."

"Not to you." Emily poked the air with her thumb. Not her hand, her thumb. It was comical to watch.

Then I heard what she said. "What?"

Emily heaved a deep sigh and pressed her cheek against the window. "Yeah, yeah. You were somewhere and she wasn't saying nice things about you tonight. Said you were crazy, obsessive, and there were other words. I know there were other words."

"I wasn't really nice to her when we went to the bathroom."

"Don't matter." Emily was firm. She shook her head in a circle. "A friend is a friend, no matter what's been done between you. I know that much. I have some good friends. Of course, they'd never go to Buds, but they're good friends. I don't like 'em sometimes, but still… I don't say bad things about 'em."

There was some merit in what she was saying, but… "What about when you just have to vent about something?"

"She ain't vented. Or… no. She didn't vent. That's it. She's seen me at my ugliest times. She's still around. Bethany Ann saw me one time with a green foliage mask on. That wasn't pretty."

"See." I flashed a grin. "You know exactly how I feel." Except what she had to say wasn't sitting well with me. It didn't feel good. None of it.

"Yep… yep…" And she was back to sleep.

I heaved a sigh of relief. Emily drunk was almost as annoying as Emily sober. Turning back to the steering wheel, I pulled onto the road and it didn't take long before I saw the campus. When I parked the car, I considered how heavy my roommate was. She was a little taller than me, but my weight.

I could handle her.

Hefting her up the stairs a few minutes later, I regretted my decision. Her head hit not one, but two doorways. Then she hit our doorway. When I caught sight of the couch, I knew I'd never be so glad to see that paisley thing in my life. Grunting one last time, I dropped Emily on the couch. Then I shut the door and sat watching Emily sleep, weighing what I needed to do. There was no real question, though. Deep down, I knew Kates was in danger.

I rubbed my hands together and knelt on the ground by Emily. Then I closed my eyes and I reached out… I broke through Emily's first layer. It was sluggish, but that was no surprise. It was the booze, but immediately underneath was a swirl of emotion. Adrenaline. I felt excitement, passion, rigidity, and a firmness inside of her. All of it was jumbled together. Then I went further and I gasped silently.

I'd always known she had a black and white perspective on life, but she was harder on herself. I felt like I was being suffocated inside of her, but I pushed further down. That's when I was hit with a wall of pain. It was masked with jealousy and insecurity. A blast of emotions hurled at me and I could almost hear the snarl. They hit me like a downpour of sleet. When I caught onto them, the hatred was physically painful. I knew I sobbed, but I just held on. I couldn't do anything else.

Hatred. Evil. Turmoil.

The adrenaline was mixed with eagerness. I knew the feeling would haunt me, but I'd found what I was looking for. The vampire was in her. Taking my time, I waded through each strand. They were all entangled together. This vampire might've spent time with a Hunter, but he was cruel. I felt how much he loved to be cruel, but then again, a Hunter was sometimes the cruelest of them all. It made sense what company he'd keep.

I managed to search through each strand. Sometimes I just got a feeling. Sometimes I got a name. Other times, I got a place or a memory. Certain emotions centered on a specific time or memory with him. Then I got an image of his cruelty, a little girl. When I heard her defeated whimper, I shed some tears. The pictures, feelings, thoughts, memories—everything swirled together and then out of the middle the word 'slayer' lashed at me.

I bolted upright and jerked away from the couch. I was hurled out of Emily. Curling into a fetal position on the floor, I was helpless to stop the tears. They just trickled down. Some of it came from the vampire. Some from the little girl, but I knew the majority were from my own wounds.

I was bleeding and raw, but I needed to find Kates.

CHAPTER FIVE

I tried to call Kates, but there was no answer. Then I thought about calling Blue, but before I could, my own phone rang. I slapped it against my ear and heard, "It is about time you called me!"

Blue sounded like she was at her wits' end.

"Girl, you need to tell me that I'm off-racket. Tell me that my senses are going sky-rocket into nomad's land. Tell me… tell me that I'm high and I've got a debt to the peyote drug lord. Please."

Blue knew better.

I sighed softly and murmured, "You should've blocked me."

"Oh… hell…" Blue groaned. "How am I supposed to block you? You're my… you're mine."

She was my sponsor. It was a bond that we weren't supposed to impede, but… situations could run amok and who knew where both of us would be. A person always hears how the 'team' is there for them, how it's all for one and one for all—it's literally true when you're empathic.

"I know," I sighed.

I could hear those wheels in Blue's head and I knew she was turning them rapidly… She asked, "You said you were going to call me. What were you calling me for?"

"Can you feel someone for me? My old friend, Kates." I didn't need any other introduction. Kates was well known, by my sponsor and the rest of the empaths. When a vampire slayer is slaughtered, empaths feel and remember it for years.

"Oh girl," Blue whispered, brokenly. "Are you sure?"

"Yes." I sat up straighter. "I can't. I'm really weak right now."

"I will, but you have to promise me."

Oh God. I waited in dread because I already knew what she was going to say. She always harped about it.

"You have to go to the next Empath meeting with me."

"Fine." I'd figure a way out of it later.

Emily grunted a snore behind me. It sounded like a train warning of its arrival, but she flipped on her stomach and the snore was muffled by the couch. I groaned and sat up straight to stretch a little, but was distracted when I heard Blue humming. I cracked a grin. I'd forgotten she did that when she needed to search for her person.

Some empaths, the really skillful ones, could close their eyes and have the person immediately. Those were the best of the best. The rest of the upper middle class could do it, but much more slowly. Blue had told me that when she first trained for this skill, she learned by feeling every person, in every room, every building, down every street before she found her target. It sounded exhausting to me and completely ludicrous. For some reason, most of the empaths liked to have this skill. They liked working on their gift (curse—as I say) and expanding it. The curse can drive a person crazy if you're unable to shield and block others.

"Oh… oh… oh… OH….. oh…"

Blue was not having an orgasm.

"Oh….. uhhuh…. uhhuh…" This was followed by some grunts. "Ummmmm….." Blue went back to her humming. "Oh, child. You're in some trouble, aren't you?" Then she said, "Davy, you need to help that girl."

"What'd you feel?" I felt a knot in my throat.

"You know that I can't tell you. What I felt within Kates is private and she chooses when to tell her friends, if she does. But I will tell you who you can call to help. She trusts him. I felt that and I already felt that she's told you."

I groaned. I already knew who she was going to say and then I heard my worst fear. "There's a Hunter in town. She trusts him. He can help you. He can help *her*."

"Why did I ask in the first place?" Holy man, I really hated that vampire.

Blue chuckled gravely. "The most gifted always search. It's an automatic radar, Davy. It continually scans without causing you the normal pain. But only the most gifted are able to do that."

I didn't need to hear that. I did not want to be one of the 'most gifted.' I couldn't keep the disbelief out of my voice. "Right."

"It's true. I haven't said anything because I'm aware of how you feel, but it's true. You are very gifted. What you can do… takes my breath away sometimes."

It took my breath away too—and not in the good way.

Emily moaned in her sleep, which was followed by another train arriving at the station. Okay, I needed to face facts. I couldn't do anything about my most cursed gift, but I could do something about Kates. "The Hunter, huh?"

"He's who you need to contact. Do you know how?"

Do I know how? I scoffed at that thought. There's always a few venues to search out a Hunter, but lucky for me—I had my roommate.

"Yeah. I'll be fine," I reassured her.

"Alright…," I could sense her unease now. "…just, I'll lower my shield to you so you can reach me if you get in trouble. I'll alert the community immediately."

That was not what we needed. If she alerted our community, the empathic community, then it might be war between the empaths and vampires.

"No, no. I'll be fine. I'll find the Hunter. We'll be fine."

"Okay. Well…. I'll be feeling you." And Blue hung up with her slightly eerie parting.

After that, I needed to wake Emily. The idea was not appealing, but I reached forward and gently patted her shoulder. "Emily. Em."

Nothing.

"Hey!" I shoved her this time.

"What? Huh?" She blinked, dazed, and struggled to focus. "Davy?"

"Do you have Roane's phone number?" She just looked at me. I snapped my fingers in front of her face and I saw the fog separate.

"Huh?"

"Luke Roane."

"Luke? Is he here?" She started to sit up, but I pushed her back down.

"He's not, but I have to call him. Do you have his number?"

"Uh…"

I saw the wheels turn slowly, but I knew she was starting to wonder why I'd need his number… and why I needed to call him. "Where's his number? I wanted to warn him about Kates. I think she might like him."

"It's in my cell phone." Her answer was predictably instant.

"And where's that?"

"My purse." She lifted her arm weakly and it dropped back down with a plop.

I saw that her arm was still through the pink purse straps. I hadn't even noticed when I carried her inside, but then again, I was a little distracted by carrying her entire body. After I snagged her phone from inside, I thumbed through the contacts and found him. It took four rings before I heard his abrupt greeting, "Who is this?"

My mouth was dry. "Emily's roommate."

"Who?"

He didn't remember my roommate? "You know, the one that your buddy bit tonight."

There was silence on the other end, long tense silence. "What do you mean?"

"I need your help. I think my friend is in danger."

"Who is this?"

Good God. "The empath!"

"Oh." He understood now. He was quiet for a moment, a long moment, and then he asked, "Your friend is in danger?"

"Yeah. I need your help."

"The slayer." He seemed to choose his words carefully.

"Kates. She's not the slayer."

"She has the powers of a slayer."

"There's a difference. She's not a slayer," I defended, heatedly. I shouldn't care this much, but being a slayer according to the new decree was illegal and it warranted instant death as punishment. The Hunters replaced the slayers. The slayer elders had agreed with the decree and so it was born.

Roane didn't respond to my argument. "Where are you?"

"At my dorm."

"With your roommate?"

"Yes." Why was this so confounding to him? "I got your number from her."

"From Emily?"

"Nevermind. Where do I meet you?"

There was silence again on his end.

"I can come to you," I cried impatiently into the phone. Why did he need to consider this? He was a Hunter. He had to help, didn't he? Although, truthfully, I wasn't sure what their job requirements were. I mostly just knew they hunted the bad vampires. I waited for a long breath and then he said abruptly, "I'll come to you. Don't leave your dorm."

He hung up immediately and Emily snored from the couch. Ignoring her, I programmed the vampire's phone number into my phone before I stood up—then I felt awkward. I didn't know what I was waiting for, but I sat at my desk and waited… and waited … and waited some more. It'd been an hour before I growled to myself. I couldn't stay in the room any longer so I left and went downstairs to the lobby. Of course, when I got there I noticed two things. It was two in the morning and Shelly was wrapped around Adam in the television lounge.

CHAPTER SIX

I tried to slip outside, but no luck.

"Davina!" Adam called out, hurried, and did my ears detect a little bit of guilt? I was pretty sure they did.

"Hey," he called again and eagerly waved a hand.

Shelly unwound her tentacles around him, but one of her arms remained on his hip. It was intimate and I knew her smirk wasn't coincidental. They both looked dressed up, but Adam had on a sleek buttoned-down black shirt that looked like it'd been ironed. He always looked nice, but this was a pay grade above that. Shelly wore a leather shirt fastened together by one big pearl button underneath her breasts. It added cleavage. Lots of cleavage. The girl knew how to dress. Even Kates would've been appreciative.

"Hi, Davy." Shelly's ruby red lips formed a perfect, unfriendly, smile.

Adam was blind. He beamed. "So… where are you going this evening?"

"More like morning, Adam." Shelly laughed and patted his arm.

If I were a vamp, my fangs would've already been out.

"Oh yeah. I didn't realize how late it was. We were just… talking. Time must've gotten away from us both." Adam smiled nervously and shuffled on his feet.

He was uncomfortable. Good. He should be.

"Are you just going out?" Shelly asked this time. Her quick eyes skimmed me up and down. I wasn't exactly dressed for a nightclub, but I knew I looked alright. How could a person go wrong with black? And it was tight. Tight always seemed to be good with guys, though that wasn't why I wore it.

"Uh…" I opened my mouth, but closed it. I wasn't sure what to say. I couldn't tell them the truth, but I was a horrible liar.

Shelly's eyes smarted. She asked, quick on the prowl, "Do you have a date?"

"A date?" Adam sounded taken aback, but he tried to hide it.

Oh yeah, bucko. I have a life besides you… wait. Was this what I wanted my future boyfriend to think? I wasn't sure.

"Davina…"

I stiffened at that word and not because it was the name I started to loathe (no one can remember Davy), but because I was hit by the same cold blast as all the other times. It was followed by a host of shivers up and down my spine. Roane was able to make my name sound like a lover's caress and as I turned to look at him, the way he strolled towards us, he looked like the perfect bad boy lover that all the good girls obsessed about. Plus, the whole supernatural predator thing molded to his form perfectly. He dressed like me all in black, but he ventured into leather land. He wore a black tee shirt over a pair of black leather pants. I never noticed how high his cheeks were, the angles seemed sharper and I realized it was because he had nearly shaved all of his hair off. He now sported a clean buzz cut and it made him look even more dangerous. I understood why Emily had a thing for him, but then again all vampires had an unnatural sex appeal.

Judging by Shelly and Adam's reactions, both were aware of it. Adam seemed to stand taller while Shelly's mouth could've dropped to the ground from her drool. Her eyes quickly darted back and forth from Roane to me. "Is this your date?"

I sucked in my breath as I waited for Roane's response, but to my surprise there was none. I twisted back, prepared to see fury or something in those emotionless coal black eyes, but there was no reaction. He watched me steadily. So I gulped again and opened my mouth, but as I met Adam's uncertain eyes I closed it with a snap. I had no idea what to say. If I said it wasn't a date, they might ask where we were headed and then what? I couldn't tell the truth. These two didn't know about that world and I didn't want them to know. Anyone who got involved with that world got hurt.

So I lied through my teeth and my fingernails cut into my palms, "Yes. It's a date."

Something slammed in Adam's eyes and I felt effectively shut out.

Shelly's smile lit up, but there was a calculating sheen there. I didn't know how I felt about that, but I wanted to know exactly what she felt. I really, really wanted to know and before I realized it, I was already inside of her. Whoa—talk about multi-layered. The girl had it all, but the top emotion was selfishness. She wanted Adam, much more than me. Underneath that, she wanted to have sex with Roane, really badly and I even felt some of her calculation how to make that happen. She planned—no! I blinked, shaken, as I ripped myself out.

Shelly had plastered a fake smile on as she oozed, "…wonderful place. I highly recommend it. Right, Davina?"

"Uh…" I was a little mortified to realize that they'd had an entire conversation. "Yes. Exactly, but maybe not." I learned long ago to always be vague when someone catches you at something. It never mattered what, just be vague. I'd never gone wrong yet and Shelly immediately supplied my question.

"The Shoilster. It's a great club, right? Your… friend said that's where you're going."

The Shoilster? That place was awful. The booths were plastic and cheap. The food looked decadent, but tasted like fish. All of it tasted like fish. Shelly was crazy. I smiled politely. "Well… yes, it's wonderful at times, but not all the time. And really, we might not even go there."

"Oh. I thought…" her eyes jumped to Roane, but to my shock, Shelly didn't say a thing.

When I turned, I saw that Roane stared long and hard at her and I recognized that look. They did that when they wanted the other person to shut up. Craig had turned that look on me enough times. I couldn't tell him to stop, not with Adam there, but I needed to do something. I might really hate Shelly, but even my enemy didn't deserve to be on the other end of one of those stares. They just held a person immobile, like their thoughts were frozen in time. In my opinion, it violated their right and so I did the only thing that I could. I violated Roane's right to privacy. I narrowed my eyes and I pushed through his shields. He had a lot of them, too many, but I got through and I read the first emotion. He was annoyed and exasperated, but I didn't think it was with me or Shelly. I pushed further and found the same fierce determination to stand and stare death down.

I blinked, belatedly, and wondered where he got his motivation from. It might come in handy with a new diet I might need… I shook my head slightly and pushed even more. Vampires were a mass of swirling emotion. I'd been in enough to get a general feel, but this felt different. There was something… I couldn't put my finger on it, but there was something different inside of him. He ran by a different set of codes than the others. I felt that and in that moment, I understood why he was the one to call. Blue hadn't said it, not directly, but Kates respected this one. There was a reason… and then I felt a cold firm hand grasp my arm and I was wrenched out of him, physically and mentally. I gasped and blinked back abrupt tears—it happened sometimes when an empath was too deep. Then I looked up into Roane's coal eyes.

He was furious. He'd been unemotional before, but he let me see that fury free and clear now. I gulped and my hand clamped onto his hand. Intending to try and yank his hold free, I couldn't. I just wrapped my fingers around his arm. He was stronger than me. He wasn't moving and I couldn't make him move. We were deadlocked and then he said tersely, underneath his breath, "Stay. Out."

"Davina?" Adam called from a distance. He was five feet away. I was the one far far away, still locked in a battle of wills with the vampire. "Davina!" Adam called again, more insistent this time.

Roane held my gaze captive. He held a dark promise in his if I didn't adhere his warning. Well—two could play at that game. "Then don't use your eye radar thing on my friends."

He blinked slowly and released my arm, but it felt like some force still held me close. If he moved his arm an inch we would've been in an embrace. He murmured, almost sensually, "She's not your friend."

"I know that. It doesn't matter. You don't do it."

His eyes judged me, like he wanted to call me a liar. "Fine. It's your back for her knife." Then he moved back, just an inch, and I felt like I could breathe.

"Davina!" Adam called again.

When I looked at Adam, I think my heart stopped. He looked utterly and completely concerned for my welfare. Shelly looked pissed off with her arms folded. Her eyes darted from Roane, to myself, and then to Adam.

"Hey…" Adam gentled his tone, but he stepped forward and touched my arm. "Are you okay? I mean…" He raised cautious eyes to Roane and quieted his tone. Little did he know that there was a vampire five feet away. "That didn't look friendly. You know?"

"I'm fine." I patted his arm reassuringly. "I promise. That was… it was just a little misunderstanding."

Roane snorted behind me.

"So, you guys are going to the Shoilster? I haven't been there. I'd like to come!" Adam exclaimed suddenly and a little bit shrilly.

"What? I mean…" Shelly was startled, but she recovered instantly. She linked her elbow through his and turned a charming smile towards us. "I mean, that'd be great. Let's go. It could be, like, a double date?"

"A double date?" Adam asked, confused, as he shook his head. "No. We'd just be… hanging out, right?"

I sent Roane a helpless look, but he just smiled tightly and turned his back. Bastard vampire. "Well… okay, but I don't know. I think. I guess, I—um—we could go for a little while?"

"Great." Shelly was all for it.

"Great." I echoed Shelly's sentiments and surprised both of us when I slammed a hand on Roane's (very) chiseled chest. We both jumped under the contact, but I gritted my teeth and grabbed his hand.

"Let's… we'll meet you there."

"Uh…" Adam muttered.

Shelly locked her hands with his. "We'll meet you there! Sounds like a plan."

They were out the door before I could blink, literally. Once they were gone, it was just me and Roane. I gulped painfully. My hand was still on his chest and I felt him laughing. "Wha…?" I turned, dazed, when I saw an actual smile on his face.

I think I just wet my pants. "Stop!"

Roane just laughed harder and shook his head. Did I mention that my hand was still plastered to his chest? I didn't think I could move it. "A double date? We're on a date? I thought you were all about keeping your friend safe, but now I don't know what's more pathetic. You and this boy that you're infatuated with or… the fact that I actually came here?" He chuckled again to himself and moved away.

My hand abruptly fell to my side. "Really? I'm pathetic?"

His laughter dissolved quickly and he sobered while he studied me a moment. Then he shook his head, almost gently, and chided, "No, it's just your pursuit of being normal."

My mouth went dry and my body went numb.

He added, impervious, "You're not normal, but you're so blind to who you are that you're willing to do anything for that boy. And he is a boy, trust me."

"I'm not blind." I didn't say anything about the 'boy' factor. "I *am* too normal."

"No, you're not." He stepped closer, unnervingly so. Then he murmured and this time it was fully sensual, "You're above normal. You just don't want to admit it."

"I have a roommate. I go to college. I skip classes. I volunteer at the hotline and I hate it! That's normal. How can that not be normal?"

"And the fact that you're telling a vampire all this?" Amusement flared in his depths, but it mingled with something else, something that sent a shiver down my spine and not one of those good ones.

"You're not normal. When you accept that, you'll accept your destiny."

My destiny?

He turned to leave, but he seemed to glide from the room. I was left behind to echo, "I'm a college student. That's my destiny… what destiny? I'm like everyone else."

But there was no one in the lounge.

"Hey!" I called out, sharply.

CHAPTER SEVEN

"Your boyfriend thinks I'm the bad guy," Roane spoke up when we parked outside of the Shoilster.

I didn't even spare him a glance. It wasn't worth it. "You are. You're a vampire. You're evil."

"He's clueless and he's in danger." Roane turned to look at me and this time I met his gaze, but my eyes quickly filtered over his shoulder to where Shelly and Adam waited beside the front entrance—talk about an imposter nightclub. It was one of those clubs that had the nicest décor, but the food wasn't cooked properly, never tasted good, and hardly ever filled a person. Yet, they arranged it nicely, complete with a garnish on the very tip of the plate so it seemed like it was worth the lavish price. It was Shelly's wet dream. It had all the trimmings, but none of the quality.

"Watch it. You're broadcasting again," Roane warned with a hint of amusement.

"Shut up!" I lashed out, harshly. "You're evil and get out of my head." I reached for the door handle, but Roane slapped a hand over mine.

I froze. I didn't dare move because his hand had a cemented hold over mine. His body brushed against mine and if he'd been human, I would've felt his breathing against my cheek. I kept my eyes down, anywhere but his. Then he remarked, "I'm not in your head and that goes both ways, Empath. You stay out of mine and I'll return the favor."

"If you call me that again, I will…" I threatened, but I caught my words.

'Don't let them know you. Don't explain anything to them!' That had been Kates' first lesson to me when I confessed I was worried a

vampire was stalking me. The other lessons… I hadn't been the one to think of setting Craig on fire, but I'd been the one to throw the match. And this one—this vampire…

"Vampire," I snarled in return and turned to let him meet my stormy eyes. "I didn't want to call you, but your name popped up in my magic eight ball. There's a reason, and I'm thinking you know what it is, so let's figure out a few ground rules."

He let go of my hand and a rush of blood swept through it. I could've sobbed from the release of pressure, but my eyes hardened. "I will not 'feel' you. You will not listen to my thoughts and after we've ditched Adam and Shelly you will help me with Kates. After that, you and I go our very separate ways."

"Gladly." It was the second time he used that word with me and the same acid dripped from his tone.

"Fine."

"Fine." Then he reached for his door and was outside before I could blink.

I took a deep breath and muttered to myself, "Okay. Calm down. Be cheerful. And just fake your way till the end." That'd been another lesson from Kates, but it hadn't pertained to vampires. I liked to be adaptable and as I strode out into the cold air, I found I could breathe a little easier. Adam gave me a tentative smile. He moved away from Shelly and stepped close. "Are you okay? You don't look like you're up for this tonight. We could always…"

"Double date some other night?"

"It's not a date or a double date, not for me anyway." Adam frowned and stepped even closer. The air was cold enough to block his body heat, but I shivered as I imagined myself pressing against him. I felt a flush in my cheeks and ducked my head. I didn't want him to see how red I was, but I caught a movement from the corner of my eye. Roane shook his head with a flash of scoffing amusement. He made a point of turning his back to me.

My cheeks were aflame now, but not from eager anticipation. I could just… I held my breath and focused hard. I wanted to piss him off, I wanted to… I only knew one way to do it, but I'd just made a promise. I couldn't sneak my way inside again or I'd have to suffer the consequences.

"Davina?" Adam distracted me when he reached out to touch my arm.

I jumped from the cool touch, but exclaimed immediately, "Oh, I'm so sorry, Adam. I wasn't… I'm sorry."

"Hey," he started to say, reassuringly, but he looked furtively at Shelly and Roane. He stopped as his eyes caught and held with Roane's.

Oh god. Roane was doing the same thing with Adam that he'd done with Shelly. He had the eye radar thing going and I could feel Adam's body freeze, immobile, as the vampire took his leisure time searching through Adam's thoughts.

I only had a few options, but I reacted without thinking. I covered the space between myself and Roane before my brain had time to scream 'Be rational!' As if I had no control over my actions, I watched my own hands grasp the front of his shirt roughly. Roane didn't have time to react before I pushed against him and slammed my lips over his. After that I felt like something unlocked inside of me. Adam was released from Roane's distraction. My eyes snapped shut and I pressed harder against Roane. As kisses went, it was forced and impersonal.

Then I felt Roane's hand slide around to the back of my neck and he took a breath before he took over the kiss. After that, all force and impersonal formality was gone within an instant. Roane's lips opened over mine and he parted mine expertly. I felt his tongue sweep inside and I gasped from the molten intrusion. He switched our places. I was lifted up and pushed against the wall as his head tilted us so our backs were partially hidden. His hand cupped the side of my face and his thumb ran over my lips as he pulled away to nip at them gently. My eyes were still closed, but I couldn't control my body. Every time he leaned close to nip at my lips, I arched into his touch, begging for more. When I heard a soft chuckle resound from him, I opened my eyes bleakly and saw a smug vampire staring at me.

All the heat, the passion that I didn't want to admit to myself, was instantly replaced with coldness. I snapped and shoved him back.

Roane went, but he went slower than I'd wanted.

I swung horrified eyes to Adam, but I saw that he was gone. Shelly must've gone with him. "They're gone."

"After that display, I doubt your boyfriend is going to show his face again."

"He's not my boyfriend." I had really wanted him to be though.

Roane said smugly, "You kissed me in front of him. You can't explain that away, Empath."

Empath! I swung my fists at him. My hand was two centimeters away from slapping his face when it was caught and held in his powerful grip. The smug smirk was replaced by cold anger. "Don't do that again."

I felt a slow shiver from his words, but I was beyond caring. "Don't ever call me that again!" I waited in thick silence before he released my hand. It dropped with a thud to my side, but I still fought from swinging my other hand.

"Fine, then you can stop calling me Vampire. My name is Luke, not Roane."

I shrugged and sniffed, "Whatever."

"Why did you kiss me?"

"Because… we made a deal. It was the only thing I could do to stop you from doing that thing again."

"That thing?" Roane—Luke—echoed with a twinge of laughter in his voice. "What do you mean by 'that thing'?"

I knew this test. It was more about me than him. He just wanted to know what I knew. "It's what you, vampires, do when you want to search inside someone's head. It's worse than what I can do. You put your eye radar on that person and they can't move so you can take your time looking through their brain index. I hate it and I really hate that Adam doesn't even know what you did. He just thinks…"

I felt like I could vomit.

"He saw you kiss me," Luke finished for me.

"Now he'll think…" I didn't know what exactly he'd think, but with a sinking heart, I knew there was nothing I could do now.

"Want to know what he thinks? I can tell you."

It must've been my imagination because I detected a small bit of sympathy in his tone. Vampires weren't sympathetic. I'd gone crazy. I lied, "No."

"He likes you. He thinks I'm a bastard, but he's worried about your welfare. He won't be deterred from the kiss. Trust me."

"Really?" The vampire was a complete contrast of emotions. I hated him, I needed him, and now—I was grateful to him.

He sighed and then swung towards the door. "Let's go."

"This place?" I still disliked this place. "We don't have to go here now. They're gone. We can go and find Kates now."

"This is where Kates is." Roane moved towards the door and a bouncer swept it open. Roane passed through like he owned the place. I was forced to reluctantly follow and when he turned down into a back hallway I knew this night had gone from bad to worse.

"Let's go!" he commanded down the hallway and then I saw him open a door.

I sighed and quickened my pace even though this went against how I usually operated. I liked to slowly wade in and get my surroundings before I made rash decisions. It hadn't been a rash decision to light Craig on fire. I'd thought and planned for weeks in advance and then the night came along. This was different. I'd been to the Shoilster, but I'd never been down a back hallway and certainly not a basement. The door was left open, but Luke was already downstairs and out of my eyesight.

"Get down here, now!"

My foot reacted first and I fumbled my way down the stairs. What I saw when I got to the end brought my jaw to the ground, almost literally.

The main floor of the Shoilster was used for dining and dancing. Not the basement. The basement looked like another secret gathering of vampires. They were everywhere. Some sat on plush red couches that lined the walls. Some stood in the middle, between two ponds that shown a sparkling reflection on the ceiling. I wondered if there were crystals or diamonds in the ponds, but then I forgot my question as my gaze caught and held on a girl in a back corner.

Kates.

She stood with a sultry smile on her face and her body was leaning suggestively towards a guy who looked like he'd love to ravish her that night. They both held crystal goblets with red liquid and I had a fleeting thought that his might hold blood, but Kates' would've had merlot. For all her dressings, she was a wine girl through and through.

I didn't know how long I stood there, but when a few vampires started to send glances my way, I decided it was time to mingle— or… just move. I moved. Like any other bar patron, I found myself at the crowded counter with no chance of heralding a bartender. It was packed. I was surprised that I'd even noticed Kates in the first place.

"Are you alone?" The question came out smoothly, too smoothly, and the blonde vampire stood tall. He was over six feet with a square jaw and sparkling blue eyes.

I smiled for different reasons. Roane had disappeared so I was alone. Then I smiled because this vampire thought I was a lost, misdirected little human who had no idea he thirsted for my blood. I felt a wave of confidence sweep through and I relaxed for the first time in awhile. Leaning back against the counter I slipped into Silvia's persona. I held a hand out. "What's your name? You look like… a Ben? No. Maybe a… Royce. Are you a Royce? Are you the sixteenth heir in a line of royal blue bloods? You dress the part. Is that custom fitted?"

I gave the vampire credit. He was startled, but he rolled easily on his heels and he returned with charm,

"It is actually. I can order something for you, if you'd like."

"But, wait—you'd have to get my measurements first, right?" My smile dazzled. "I know this gig, forwards and backwards. You're not getting my blood."

That got his attention. If he'd had breath, I would've given myself a pat on the back for stealing it away. He didn't so I didn't pat myself on the back, but it didn't matter. I saw his nostrils flare and my heart sunk. I'd just become the next big challenge for this vampire and I knew how that road traveled.

"Don't," I said sharply as I held a hand up. "I lit the last vampire on fire who thought I was a challenge for him to bleed. I'll do it again and it won't take nearly as long this time. That's my warning to you."

"Kade," Roane decided to join the conversation from… I glanced around. I had absolutely no idea where he materialized from, but his presence snapped Kade into order.

"Lucas," Kade returned as he waited for his leader to speak. The blonde Casanova instantly stood straighter and waited for his command.

"Leave." That was all Roane said and Kade turned to leave, but he stopped mid-turn and raked his eyes over me. "I like you." He pounded Roane on the chest before he finally turned to leave.

Roane studied me intently. "Do I dare ask what that was about?"

"No."

"Okay." Roane was easy.

"I saw Kates."

Roane narrowed his eyes, but he didn't say anything. Instead, he signaled for a drink and just like that—he got one. I glowered. "Could get me one, but no…"

He lifted a second finger and I felt better when a beer was pushed into my hand. I didn't bother to say thanks. "What's the plan?"

"You wanted help. I brought you to your friend. I thought you were worried about her."

I flushed and raised my beer to him. "You know that's not all there is to the story. I thought she was in trouble. My…," I hesitated. "My source said to contact you so I did."

"Your magic eight ball. Tell me, how'd your magic eight ball mention me? Was it by name?"

"You're making fun of me."

"No," he rejected quickly. "Unlike you, I know why you contacted me, but I'm just wondering how much you actually know."

"I know." I didn't, but I wasn't about to let him know that. "I know plenty."

Roane chuckled. "You know nothing."

"Oh, really?" I turned to face him squarely. I even put my beer on the counter to let him know that I meant business. "You think I know nothing? Well… I know enough, Vampire."

I said the word and I said it hotly. I dared him to call me on it. Oh yes, I'd call him Vampire if I wanted.

Roane smiled coolly and returned, "What do you know, Empath?"

I felt hot, angry, but I'd started us down this road. I'd see it through. "I know something big is going down. There's a whole crap load of vampires here and I don't think that's normal for Benshire. I know that there was a girl who killed herself the other night and a whole host of too many vampires were in attendance. There were two on the roof with her and six on the ground. I think whatever's going on has something to do with why Kates is here because I'm not stupid enough to think she's actually here for me."

There. I was out of breath. I'd said it all. I felt my skin starting to crawl before Roane replied cautiously, "You're smart for an empath., but maybe too smart? Maybe you know too much for your own good?"

My eyes bulged and my throat went dry, but what did I do? I took a drink of my beer when I heard the very words that I'd feared coming from a vampire. Those words were never followed by anything good.

CHAPTER EIGHT

What do you do when you're in a room of vampires and the most dangerous one tells you that you know too much? You bolt. What did I do? I hyperventilated. "Oh yeah? You think I can't handle all of this?"

"Relax," Roane chided softly as he moved closer.

I tensed, but he only placed his drink on the counter behind me. I waited for him to move back, but he didn't. Then I hyperventilated a little bit more…

"I told you, relax." Roane shifted closer and his chest was nearly pressed against me with an arm tucked around me. To the outside observer, we were a couple on the quick way to a dark corner. To my inside observer, I was pretty sure I might've wet my pants.

'It's not him. It's not him,' I chanted to myself.

Roane chuckled softly against my cheek. "You're right. It's not me. It's your ex."

My eyes flew wide open—I'd closed them without realizing it, but I caught my breath when I saw Roane watching me knowingly, amused, and did I detect some sympathy too? My hand tightened around the beer bottle. It was my only weapon of defense.

"You're freaked out about all vampires because of one bad seed."

"You're all bad seeds."

"True, but most of have us enough control and self-discipline. We have carnal desires, but we don't act on them. If we did vampires wouldn't be a secret to 90% of the world's population."

True, but… they were still evil. I took a nervous sip of my beer, but I didn't taste it. In fact, as I felt the lightened bottle, I realized that either it had evaporated or I'd drunk most of it already. I wet my dry lips and hoped it had evaporated. "What… what did you mean before when you said that I know too much?"

"You do." Roane tucked his hand that had rested on the counter behind my back and pulled me close. We were now flush against each other.

Craig was the reason why I was feeling this jittery, hot flash, shivering reaction. It had nothing to do with this vampire.

Roane's breath tickled my cheek. "There are a lot of vampires here and there is a reason. You're right. I'd been hoping your friend was here for you. I doubt it, though. That's why I brought you here."

I was dumbfounded… and a little woozy.

"Do you see her?" Roane urged me forward. We were embracing now, but he tilted my head to his shoulder where I was able to prop my chin up and then my eyes went wide when I saw what he wanted.

Kates was grinding against her vampire, but I didn't see lustful Kates. She was on the prowl and I saw a predator glint in her sapphire eyes. She didn't move thick with desire. She was alert, primed and it didn't sit well with me.

Roane felt my tension and he nuzzled underneath my ear. "She's not here for you. She's not even here for the same reason the rest of us are here. She's here because she's about to do something that I don't want her to do."

"Why?" My whole body grew numb from the shock.

"You know the decree that was approved by both boards."

It was the one where hunters replaced slayers. Gulping, I knew where this was going.

"Her mother was ripped to shreds because she violated the decree. That power went to your friend. She was branded because of that. Every vampire will know she's got slayer power, but if she does what I think she's here to do—you know what will happen."

That was the problem. "Please? Just…" '…*don't kill her.*'

To my surprise, Roane didn't respond right away. His hand cupped the back of my neck. "You dropped your shield."

I had, but I hadn't done it on purpose. '*Please don't hurt her. Please… she's… she saved my life.*'

His eyes bore into mine. "I'm a marked Hunter. You know I can't."

"What do I do?"

"You save her life. You return the favor and you make sure she doesn't do what her carnal desires are thirsting for. Make sure she doesn't kill any vampires or you know what'll happen to her." He moved back an inch and signaled for two more drinks. He replaced my empty bottle with a full one. "You've seen up close what Hunters will do to anyone who violates the decree."

I closed my eyes as I saw Craig on fire, his face twisted and angry. I could still smell the charred skin and I couldn't repress a grimace. My eyes flew open when I felt Roane tip my bottle up. My mouth opened automatically and the cool liquid helped wash some of the bad memories away. I swallowed and held my breath when Roane brushed his thumb over my lips. He held my gaze, but I knew he wasn't doing the eye radar thing on me. I'd put my shield back in place, but he wet his lips. "I have enough on my plate. I can't worry that a slayer is going rogue. Take care of her, take care of your friend or… you know what I'll have to do."

Talk about no pressure. Save your friend or she'll die a horrible violent death. Yeah… I downed the rest of my beer. "Yeah… yeah, I can do that." I highly doubted it.

My eyes wandered to Kates, but when I couldn't find her, Roane supplied, "She just took a guy out the back door. If you hurry, you can get there before my guys."

I was forced to do what he bid so I shoved away from him and swept through the crowd. My body calmed a little as I moved further away, but it also grew cold. I hadn't realized how I'd been cocooned by Roane…. I caught sight of the red exit sign and pushed past three vampires that stalked towards it. I hardened my jaw and vowed to do what I needed to do, but when I pushed out the back door I stopped dead in my tracks.

Kates was sharing a smoke with the vampire and laughing. I'd expected—not this. Before I could react, the door slammed shut behind me.

"Davy?"

Oops. I smiled sheepishly. "Uh… hey. I didn't know…"

Kates stared at me, long and hard, and then flicked her cigarette on the ground. "If you tell me that you didn't know I was here, I will skin you alive."

"I knew you were and there are three vampires on the other side of this door that know you're here too." I'd be awful under torture.

Kates rolled her eyes. "Honey, every vampire in that bar knows I'm here. I'm a branded slayer, remember?"

Okay. This wasn't going how I thought it would.

"This is Cherry," Kates introduced with a back wave. "Cherry, this is my best friend, Davy."

"You're the Empath."

The way he made it sound, it was like I was the only one. There were nearly a hundred thousand of us in the world, but I was probably the only one stupid enough to meander into a vampire bar twice in one night.

Kates frowned at him. "Yeah, she's empathic. What of it?"

His quick eyes snapped to hers and read the warning. He straightened and ran a hand through his auburn curls then he flashed a charming smile. "No, she's not just empathic. She's the empath that was cozying up with the Hunter."

"What?" Kates whirled to me. Her mouth didn't drop, but I felt her bristling in shock. Kates hated being surprised.

The Hunter. That made him sound like he was famous or something, but then I realized he was famous in the vampire community. All hunters were known. "I—it wasn't like that."

"Sure," he scoffed with a knowing smirk.

Kates looked between us. "Okay." She turned and pressed a kiss to the corner of his mouth. "I'll be seeing you."

He didn't respond, but seemed to melt into the shadows as Kates grabbed my elbow and walked me out to the street and across to the next block. "Kates, I—" I started.

She hissed, "Not yet. Not here."

I was left with little choice but to follow. After we walked down another three blocks and hailed a taxi, Kates started as soon as the taxi's door was shut, "What were you thinking? You don't show up at a bar like that, not alone."

"I wasn't alone and hello—you took me to the first one, remember?"

"I was there! You weren't alone. And what do you mean, you weren't alone?"

"I went with the Vam—," I shot a fevered look at the taxi driver. "I went with Roane."

"Who?"

"Luke Roane, you know… the one that you wanted me to talk to in the first place."

Comprehension flashed and she sat back, slightly appeased. "Why?"

"Um… I thought you were in trouble. I felt it. I did my thing and his name came up. I was told to get a hold of him and he'd know what to do. He could help you."

"I'm not in trouble. What do you mean you did your thing? You didn't—that's private, Davy!"

If the taxi driver was listening, he'd think we were both crazy. "I didn't! Blue did and she told me to call Roane."

"What? Why?"

I shrugged. "She said that you respect him or something. I don't know. She said he was the one to call about this."

I waited for more confusion, but to my surprise there was just silence. I stole a look and saw that Kates looked contemplative. "Do you? I mean, do you respect him?"

She threw me a cold look. "That's private. It's not your business or your silly sponsor's. I think that whole thing is just… you don't need their help anymore. You're doing fine just by yourself. Why do you keep talking to her?"

"Not this again." I crossed my arms and scooted low in the seat.

"You don't need help. They get in your head and mix everything up. It's not good, Davy."

"You're just pissed off because someone might know a little more of your inner workings than you do, Kates."

Silence. Complete, utter, death defying silence.

"How dare you!" Kates seethed. I felt her body bristling from unspent fury.

I'd done the deed. I'd gone where both of us knew I should never go again. The truth is that Kates had more baggage than I could ever feel my way through. I suspected that Blue had only done a quick sweep of what made Kates go boom.

"Emotional baggage? I'm not the one who lit a vampire on fire!"

The taxi jerked. I met his gaze in the rearview mirror and he looked panicked. Correction: he looked like he was about to kick us out. "Ex-nay on the ampire-way."

"Screw that! And screw you, *Daveeena*. Do you even know what you were doing coming to the Shoilster? I thought you hated Roane. You hate all vampires and then I hear that you're snuggling up to one? And it's a Hunter! Really? Of all of them?"

"Kates," I tried to assuage, but I already knew it wouldn't work. "I'm sorry, but I'm not sorry. I don't think you're here to be my friend. I'm not stupid, Kates. I know that a crap load of vampires are in town. You didn't come because I saw that girl kill herself. You came for all of the vampires."

The taxi slammed on his brakes and neither of us was surprised. Normal people would've slammed against the seats from the abrupt stop, but not us. We reached out, held ourselves in place, and continued the argument.

"You're telling me what kind of friend I am? Is that what this is about? Is that why you came to the Shoilster? Because I'm a shitty friend?"

"No…" Good gracious. For such a kick ass tough chic, she was sensitive. "Look, I'm just…"

"Get out! Get out! Get out!" The driver twisted around in his seat and gripped a steel bat in his right hand.

We didn't blink. We got out and as the taxi shot off, Kates yelled, "You're right. I didn't come for you. I came because all the freaking blood-thirsty vampires are here, but do you even know why they're in town? You have no idea because this isn't your world. It's my world, Davy!" She breathed in and out raggedly.

"What are you talking about?" I asked, perplexed. Our arguments never made sense. "I don't even… What?"

"You're right! I didn't come for you. You were just my excuse. I'm a horrible, horrible friend," Kates nearly screamed.

She was irrational. I wasn't much better when I said things like this, "No, you're not. You're just… your mom was a slayer and you saw her die. All that power went to you and they all know you're a slayer, but you can't do what you're supposed to do and you can't do anything about it—except you have this weird thing with hooking up with vampires. I don't get that. You're protective about that world, which you can be because you know how I hate vampires, but…" What else could I say? I didn't know what I was trying to say. "I'm rambling. I ramble when I have an idea, but I lose the idea and you're here and I'm here and… I don't know what we're fighting about."

Kates snorted. "Just call someone to pick us up, would you?"

I took out my phone, but I caught myself. Who could I call?

"What?" Kates growled.

I waved the phone around. "Who do I call? If you're going to haul off on me again, I don't want to call Adam or…" I had no one else.

"What happened to Love Bit and Twice Not Shy?"

I groaned at the name, but it was fitting. "Emily's out for the count."

"She passed out?"

"She passed out."

I caught a fleeting grin before Kates turned her back to me and eyed the empty street. We were nowhere. We were somewhere, but I had no idea where we were so we were nowhere. Kates gestured to a street sign. "We're at Emerson and Keeley Ave. Call someone and tell them to pick us up here."

I sighed and I had no choice. I called The Vampire.

CHAPTER NINE

"Empath," he greeted as he pulled over and unlocked the doors of his black car. I was horrible with recognizing makes and models, but I knew it was black. As I got in the front seat, I saw that it was new, like new new, like next year new. The seats were made up of black leather and they were still slippery. I almost wooshed off when Kates climbed into the back seat.

"Thanks." I felt stiff as I reached for the seatbelt. "I see our truce is over with, Vampire?"

"You don't have to bother with the seatbelt." He shifted gears and shot back onto the street. "I'm taking my cues from you. You called me 'Vampire' in your head when I pulled up."

"Huh?"

Kates just snorted.

"I have vampire reflexes, Empath. We won't get into an accident."

"What does that mean?"

"It means that he can go fast and still land on his feet, just like a freaking cat. Didn't you know? All vampires have nine lives," Kates drawled from the back. She was still pissed.

I sighed.

Roane murmured, "Vampires have one life. It's called immortality."

Kates met his gaze in the rearview mirror. "Is that so? Here I thought you were the one that took away their immortality, right? You hunt them. Or did I get that wrong?"

"Takes one to know one…" The words were so smooth, so chilling, and deadly…

I had no idea what that was, where that came from, but something else was in the car with us. As I looked between Roane and Kates,

I knew it was something between them and it was something specific. I held my tongue, though. I knew that I did not want to step sideways into whatever they were in…

"You have something against vampires, Kates? I wasn't aware of that."

I needed to give him his due. He could hold his own against my nolstage.

Kates choked on something. "Please. We both know what I have against vampires and it ain't a grudge, Hunter."

"That's right. You and Cherry go way back. How long exactly?"

Kates was silent, the very scary quiet when I knew she was about to explode… any second now…

Roane slowly rolled his knuckles over the steering wheel. He was in control, perfect control. "You don't know him. You met him tonight and you had every intention of killing him."

"You don't know that! You don't know anything!" Kates came unhinged. She jerked upright and slammed against my seat. She was so furious. Kates always looked sultry. She was the sexy one of us, but just then her heavily made up make-up looked clownish on her. It looked wrong. That's when I knew that what Kates was doing was wrong.

Their argument passed over me, but I tuned back in to hear Kates shout, "—who made you judge and jury? You're a Hunter. You kill them and you enjoy that. That makes you an animal in my eyes. You're no more above the rest of them, but you like to think you are—"

"—an animal?" Roane narrowed his eyes dangerously and replied, silkily, "I'm the animal, Kates? I died. I came back as a vampire. You're a human. You have a choice in the matter. You have a soul."

"A soul." Kates threw herself back in the seat, disgusted. She glanced to the window and muttered underneath her breath, "What is that anymore?"

"Okay." I sat up and ignored the chilling glance from the vampire and turned around. I even ignored how Kates refused to look at me and how her back was perfectly poised to make me feel insignificant.

"You're stupid."

I caught the slight jerk of Kates' eyebrows.

"You can sit there and ignore me, but I know you're listening."

"Tell me, o wise best friend, why am I so stupid?"

"Are you killing vampires?"

"Like I'm going to have this heart to heart with you when *he's* in the car. Not to mention, why did you call him? I thought you hated the guy. Now you've got him on speed dial? I still can't believe that you showed up with him."

I ignored that. "Are you killing vampires? And we've been over that—I had to."

Kates scorched me with those sapphire eyes and I gulped. "I am not talking about this with him in the car—with him in any close vicinity at all. And what if I was? I'm not saying that I am, but what if I was? So what, Davy! I'm a slayer. It's what I was born to do. You don't know what it's like to have this thing inside of you, this darkness or something. I am programmed on the inside to do one thing. Kill vampires. I'm not allowed because some stupid decree made a decision that they could patrol their own. Well, that's just…" She trailed off, almost sad.

"You don't think I might know a little bit about that? I can feel inside of people. Remember what it was like in the beginning, before I upped my blocking levels? It was hell, Kates. You should remember that. I had this thing that came from inside of me and I couldn't control it. I do understand a little bit about what you're talking about." I felt wrung out just talking about it, but I remembered those first few years. I would do anything to not remember them.

The air was thick. I heard the swish of the car's wipers and a part of me realized that it had started to rain, but I concentrated on Kates, just Kates. She was so still with her face turned towards the window. I glanced at her reflection and wasn't surprised to see a lone tear trickle down the side of her face.

"I don't care what you're doing. I just can't lose you and I know that if you are doing what I feel is taboo to talk about right now—then just stop it. Okay?"

Kates sniffed. That was rare.

"Fuck off." That was the real Kates.

I fell back in my seat and glimpsed my dorm through the window. Roane turned the car into the parking lot and slowed to a halt just before the quad's archway. As soon as we had stopped, Kates scrambled out and slammed the door. The car rocked from her force.

"That went… stupendous," I sighed.

Roane shifted the car into park and turned it off.

I didn't care if the car sprouted roots and became a tree. I just knew that my butt had no desire to follow a pissed off vampire slayer, especially when my roommate was probably still sleeping.

"She heard you. That's all that I really hoped for the night."

Huh?

Roane added, "She knows that I know what she's doing. She knows that you know and that you're worried for her. That's all we can hope. If she stops, then good for all of us. If she doesn't, then it's my problem. Not yours."

"I didn't follow anything you just said."

"You don't need to. You tried. That's all you can do."

"You're very supportive for being a vampire." I couldn't stop the sneer. Then I felt the same coldness from before. I looked up and gulped when I felt his coal eyes on me. They were colder than normal.

"You need to get over your ex. Things will go a lot smoother for the both of us when you do."

"What are you talking about? I felt that Kates was in trouble and for some screwed up reason, I got you to help me. Whatever.

We both saw how well the 'slaying intervention' just went. You and me, that's never going to happen again." I felt brave and bold, but a part of me trembled on the inside. I just didn't know what or why…. Then I burst out, "Why was your name in her head? Why did I have to call you? You're the one…" I called her executioner. That's what I did. So… why? That question burned me.

I was surprised to hear sympathy in his voice. "I know that she's breaking vampire law. I was in her head because she fears me and she needs me. I'm the one that has to stop her."

"But…"

"You're the friend who can help me do that. No one else can do that."

That explained some of it, but there was other weird stuff going on too. "Why are there so many vampires?"

"Because…" He trailed off. For the first time, I didn't sense all of his attention on me. It felt liberating and yet, I got a sudden sick feeling. He was the primal predator. When their attention wasn't on the prey that meant it was on some other prey, something worse…. He blinked, once, and the spell was gone. His fierce eyes turned back on me and I felt all that attention once again. "Does it matter?"

"I think it does." My throat was dry.

"Talk to your friend. Plead with her again and maybe you and I won't have to do this again."

He'd dismissed me. Just like a flip of a switch. "And here I thought you were a little more human than most vampires. You proved me right. You're just as much of a dick as most guys I know. Thanks for that, it's very human of you." I threw open my door and stalked off. When I reached my dorm I glanced over my shoulder and saw that he was gone. Ass.

As I moved through the first lobby and darted up the stairs, I paused before my dorm door. I didn't know if I could handle what was on the other side. I was tired. The hallway smelled of moldy toast and I grimaced when a bad aftertaste formed in my throat. I stood there for awhile and took a deep breath.

The moldy toast had nothing on Kates.

When I bolstered up the courage and opened my door, I wasn't surprised to find Kates packing a bag. I didn't even comment when I saw a pair of my jeans in her bag. Instead, I closed the door, sat by my desk, and heard the snores from Emily.

Kates clenched her jaw tighter and threw more clothes in the bag. After a minute of silence, she screamed. "Nothing? Really? Nothing?"

"Are you leaving town?" It was all I asked because I wanted her gone. I wanted her away from him. It didn't bother me one bit if she was mad at me. This was for her own good.

Kates studied me as she twisted her hands in a sequined halter top. She loved that shirt and I knew she'd regret ripping it so I stood and gently took it away. She let me, which surprised me. "Are you doing what he says?"

"…yes…" She turned away as the admission slipped out.

I knew it, but hearing it was different. I already felt like I needed a time out. "Can you stop?"

"No."

"Why not?"

"Because…" Kates turned back to face me. I saw the tears swimming in her eyes and I blinked back my own. "…because they killed my mother, because they're trying to tell me that I can't be who I am, because they're my whole world. I know what'll happen to me if I'm caught and he knows that I am. I finally know that he knows."

"Leave town." 'Get away from him.'

"There are others like him. There are other hunters."

"You can go to one of my meetings with me. It might do you good."

"I'm not empathic." She dipped her head and I heard a chuckle.

I nudged her toe with mine. "It doesn't matter. The meetings are supposed to help anybody and everybody…Why do you do it? Do you know why, I mean, really why? It might help if you understand it."

"Right. I'm going to go to a shrink and tell them that I can't stop killing vampires. I won't get thrown in an asylum at all."

"What about Blue? She knows about this stuff. She makes me talk to her about my stuff all the time."

"Oh, I can see that one. Your sponsor and me as roommates, because she doesn't know how much I hate all that crap she makes you do."

Blue did know. Blue knew a lot more, but I wasn't going to voice it. "Try it."

When I heard my phone peel, I already knew who was on the other end. "Hello, Blue. You know we were talking about you."

"I'm not a damn mind reader. I felt a question. What's the question?"

Blue would never cease to amaze me. "Can Kates come and stay with you for awhile? She's got… some things to talk about."

"I'm making breakfast. Have her pick up some coffee on the way. I like the pumpkin spice latte."

"Blue says—"

"I heard." Kates didn't look too sure… "I go and talk to her and this is how I'm supposed to get help? It's just like that? That's too easy, Davy, even for you."

It was all I could think of. "He won't know where you are."

"If he wants to know, he'll know."

"Kates…" I wasn't sure if I should ask, but another question kept nagging me. "Why are all the vampires here?"

"Because they have fairy tales just like us. We have Santa Claus or the Easter Bunny, but they have the Immortal."

So much of that statement made no sense. "They *are* immortal."

"Not *their* immortality. It's the Immortal, as in a human who has immortality."

Huh?

CHAPTER TEN

I was dumbfounded and clueless and I *still* hadn't moved from my desk chair, even after my butt had gone numb an hour ago. That was how long it took for Kates to explain about the Immortal. Then she explained again. And again.

I was still confused. "So you're saying…"

Kates threw up her hands. "You're not normally stupid."

The insult bounced off of me. "They think this Immortal—"

"—a human who has immortality." Kates rolled her eyes.

"—has blood that they want? I don't… why the fairytale analogy?"

"Oh my God! For real? You can understand my sick twisted insides, but you don't get this?"

"Explain it again." And this time, I'd pay attention and not get lost on the idea of a human who has immortality or the fact that the vampires want immortality. They already had it so why… I was lost again.

"I'll break it down. Vampires need blood to live, right?"

I nodded, but it wasn't entirely true. They could go without, but would go crazy.

"There's only one Immortal in the world at a time and they have special fluids inside of him/her/whoever."

"Okay…" Still confused.

"When a vampire drinks the blood of an immortal, they get the juice of life."

"Juice of life?"

Kates threw herself backwards on my bed. "I had no idea this would be that hard."

"Again." I nodded emphatically with knowledge-absorbing eyes. I'd lap up the information like I was a dog drinking water. Something told me that Kates was ready to storm out of there, whether I understood or not. It was that same something that told me I needed to know this stuff.

"Vampires need blood. The Immortal has life in its blood. When a vampire drinks her/his/its blood they don't need blood to survive anymore. They've got the juice that keeps that Immortal alive. They won't thirst for blood anymore and that has some serious consequences."

I couldn't worry about the consequences or what the significance meant. I was still wrapping my head around a vampire's fairytale. "So if they drink the Immortal's blood, they don't need blood? At all? They're not hungry? How many times do they have to drink from the Immortal?"

Kates shrugged and stretched languidly. "I have no idea. No vampire has ever drunk from the Immortal that I know of. We need food, right? It's like if we took one big bite of some magical Wheaties. The magical cereal would stay inside of us and we would never need to eat again, ever."

"I'd still want to eat other things." Spaghetti. Lasagna. Anything with pasta or chicken… I loved burgers too. I should love salads.

"We're human. They're vampires. I'm sure not all blood tastes the same, but think of it this way. They're supreme meal is human blood. The decree says that they can't drink humans anymore, except when they sneak a taste like from LoveBit and Still Passed Out Here." Kates lazily gestured to Emily, who rolled over and snorted a snore in response. "But that's wrong too. If they get a taste of the Immortal's blood, they no longer need to lavish up whatever crappy blood they have to drink now. They're not like us. We like food. A lot of vampires have a love/hate thing with blood. Ask your new buddy, Roane. I bet he's one of the vampires who detests having to drink blood or detests how much he misses human blood. Get the tragic stuff?"

Not at all, but I nodded anyway with wide eyes. And he wasn't my buddy. He'd never be my buddy.

"I'm surprised your sponsor hasn't called to check on me or something."

"She knows that we're still talking," I mumbled automatically as my mind was still trying to wrap around Kates' magical Wheaties metaphor.

"Say that again?"

I blinked and saw the stillness in Kates. She looked… well, she looked like Kates again: pissed, tired, and raring for a fight. "She probably figures that we're still talking and that's why she hasn't called." I was a bad liar.

"Is she permanently in tune with you?"

I couldn't ignore that Blue had called before when we'd both been thinking of her. Blue was my sponsor. She was always alerted towards me, but that didn't necessarily mean she was inside all the time. Actually, she was hardly ever inside of me. I had some superior shields to the best vampire or empath, but I couldn't tell Kates that. If Blue wasn't tuning into my radio, that meant she was tuned into Kates'. Judging by the stormy expression in Kates' cobalt eyes—I swallowed what I'd been about to say and lied, "Yes, she is."

Relief and pity flashed in Kates' gaze, but the tension quickly left her. "I should go…" Kates stood reluctantly and glanced uneasily towards the door.

It took a few more minutes, but after she left I glanced at the clock and saw it was close to five in the morning. With a long drawn-out yawn, I used the bathroom and readied for bed. Then I closed my eyes in blissfulness as I crawled into my bed. Heaven. Emily snorted, but it didn't faze me. Nothing fazed me… I felt sleep creep into my limbs and before long; I knew I drifted off to sleep…

I felt the heat first. It blasted me and my eyes shot open to see that I was back on the roof and the girl who had jumped to her death was in front of me. I felt a shiver travel down my spine and then glanced over my shoulder for the vampires, except there were none. I closed my eyes and sensed out, but I didn't feel any beneath us either. It was also warm out. I'd been on that roof that night and it hadn't been warm.

"Davina…" she called to me.

I don't know why, but I clamped my eyes tighter together. Something told me not to open them. If I did, I'd see something I didn't want to or hear something I didn't want to…

"Look at me," she commanded and my eyes popped open. I had traitorous eyes.

She had stood on the edge with tears glistening on her cheeks that night. There was no sadness now. Instead, I saw urgency, but she was calm. She had been turned half away from me, but she faced me squarely. She wore the same white dress that billowed around her slender frame. A warm gust of wind teased the ends of her auburn curls, but she didn't have inflamed cheeks this time. They were pale, as they might've always been. Her hazel eyes were framed by thick, rich eyelashes, but that's not what mesmerized me.

She spoke with her eyes.

"You don't… you can't talk to me normally?" I was fascinated, but a little weirded out.

She smiled softly, but her mouth didn't move. "This is your dream. You make up the rules."

I blinked. "Uh… what?"

She smiled gracefully. "Reach out to me, Davina. Reach out to me…"

"I did that night."

"Reach out to me…" Her eyes were misted now, haunted.

I couldn't breathe.

"You know what I'm trying to tell you. Reach out to me so you can understand now."

"Understand what?" Chills blasted me. I felt goose bumps up and down my arms. A cold breeze wafted against my neck and the hairs on my back stood upright.

She glided closer to me with a hand outstretched.

I got one of those creepy feelings as if I was watching a horror movie play out in front of me. Or if I was in a horror movie and I was the next victim to die.

"I chose."

I snorted. "You chose to die that night. Good for you."

"No." She shook her head and those perfect lips still didn't move. "I chose you."

I gasped and jerked upright. I couldn't breathe. Something wasn't letting me breathe. My eyes popped open and I found myself in bed, heaving frantically for air. I was drenched in sweat with my blankets on the ground. Sunlight blinded me and I gasped, covering my eyes. It didn't help the splitting headache that had formed at the back of my head.

"Morning."

I saw Emily at her desk, wearing her white terry-cloth robe with her bunny slippers. She'd just showered, but she looked like she'd been hit by a bus that reversed and did it again. Judging by the bags underneath her eyes and the drooped shoulders, I knew my roommate was feeling her first hangover.

"Morning," I rasped out and lifted my arms. I felt like anchors were tied to both of them and they fell abruptly back on my lap.

"You had a nightmare. You were screaming and you threw all of your covers off. I covered you up three times, but you kept kicking them off. I gave up." Emily lifted a wary shoulder and turned back to the book she had opened in front of her.

It was worse than a nightmare, but I wasn't in the sharing mood. I wasn't even sure if my voice sounded normal. I just hoped that I hadn't wet my pants. Then I sniffed the aroma of coffee and quickly saw her mug beside her. "What is that?"

"Huh?" Emily sounded like a zombie, sluggish and nearly catatonic.

"You have coffee?"

She looked at it, but pushed it away. "You can have it. I'm not feeling all that great." Her cheeks pinked and she ducked her head in shame. Oh, my very sheltered roommate.

"What are you doing all day today?" I asked when I finally got the energy to get out of bed and grab the mug. The mug warmed my hands, which was good. They were sickly cold and covered in sweat, but my pants didn't smell so I knew I hadn't messed myself.

"I think I'm sick. I'm just going to stay in and watch movies all day. You?"

"I'm huh…" I was dumbfounded. Emily never took sick days, even when she was sick enough to be admitted to a hospital.

She coughed. "I'm supposed to work at the hotline booth at the convention today. Do you think you could fill in for me?"

I was completely speechless. Me. Hotline. Convention. Not happening. "I quit, remember?"

"You still have to make that official with Mr. Moser so you didn't. Besides, I'm supposed to work with Adam today."

"Sold!" I was a whore. Not really, but now that I knew Kates was safe I could get back to my first objective: Adam. After what he'd witnessed last night, I knew I had damage control to do.

"Besides, I don't want to take the chance that I'll see Luke at the convention. I look awful today."

I looked at her, horrified. It was a good thing she wasn't looking back otherwise she would've seen the guilt that I had branded on my entire face. Oh god. With everything that had happened last night, I'd almost forgotten about Emily's ramblings. She'd been in an altered state, but the truth came out and I knew she had a thing for him.

"Hey, Emily…" Really? What was I going to say? 'Don't like Luke Roane because he's a vampire and he's a dick? Don't like him because he hunts other vampires and kills them? Or maybe… don't like him because I kissed him in front of Adam and Luke Roane knows that I'm empathic?' I'm sure they'd all go over well.

"What?" Emily asked, impatient.

"Uh… nothing. I'll go to the convention for you."

"I know." She made it sound like it'd been inevitable. "You gotta be there in twenty minutes."

That's when I looked at the clock and thought my heart stopped beating. It was 1:39. I hit the ground running.

CHAPTER ELEVEN

Our school held a volunteer convention on the main lawn of the campus. It was surrounded by brick buildings and a few ponds on three sides. Statues were displayed randomly over the lawn, but I knew it wasn't by accident when the crisis hotline booth was placed next to the angel statue. She was in gray stone, her two eyes watched wherever you went, and her tight curls were in dire need of a new perm. The wings had been sculpted to arch upwards as if she were about to push into the air and fly away.

She freaked me out.

I dropped into one of the vacant seats behind our table and announced when someone sat beside me, "I named her Eileen."

"Uh… okay."

Did my ears detect? I looked and was rewarded. Emily had sweetened the pot with Adam, but I hadn't let myself hope. Now, I did.

Adam looked refreshing in a soft blue sweater and a pair of tan corduroys. Both molded to his tall form while his chestnut curls accentuated his yummy almond eyes. I almost wanted to eat him. If I'd been a vampire, I might've ignored the decree.

"You named her Eileen?" He smiled and ducked his head. "Uh… oh… kay. Um, where's Emily? I'm not complaining or anything, but I thought I had the afternoon block with her."

"Emily's sick." I turned and stared at Eileen for a moment. Was it my imagination or did she seem to grow before me?

"Oh. Okay. So… um… you and that guy, huh?"

Just like that, Eileen lost her appeal. I closed my eyes and cleared my throat. I knew I had damage control to do, but I hadn't known it would start this soon. The need to deceive was itching and so I itched it. "He has a girlfriend that was there. They had a tiff and he wanted to make her jealous. I didn't want to… I wanted to tell you, but then all of the sudden she was in front of the club and I kissed him. I know, I know. It wasn't smart of me or anything, but when a friend asks for a favor who am I to say no?" I held my breath. When I saw the instant relief flash in those adorable almond eyes, I expelled it.

"Oh so… you and him aren't…?"

"No. God no! No." I couldn't emphasize that enough.

"That's um… that's good to hear because…"

I watched in disbelief as Adam opened those perfectly formed lips and spoke in slow motion. It took a moment before the sound hit my ears, but I heard, "…go on a date? Maybe tonight?"

"Yes!" I shouted and instantly cowered back in my chair. Never appear too eager. Kates hadn't taught me that lesson. I'd learned it on my own, but sometimes I couldn't control myself.

Adam looked taken aback. He paused a second before he nodded. "That sounds great. I was thinking of the Alexander Restaurant. It's supposed to have good food."

I hoped my drool was kept in check. I had no idea where the Alexander Restaurant was and I didn't care about good food. We could go to the Shoilster for all I cared. A date with Adam! I'd die happy when I told Shelly Witless.

"Are you guys from the hotline? Do you have any pamphlets?"

Adam immediately started his perfect volunteer thing. I was content to sit back and daydream about our perfect date, listening to his voice drone on until the guy was done with his questions. A few more people came over and Adam was eager to answer questions. I was eager not to. I considered us a good team.

"…that girl died, right? Wasn't someone there?"

My chair tipped forward and I almost went flying into the table. My eyes shot open to see whoever was talking with Adam. The guy looked like an average student. He could've been Adam's twin dressed in Abercrombie, but it wasn't the sight of him that sent my alarms buzzing. I felt him. He was a vampire. In fact, the girl who had stopped before him and the first guy had been vampires too. I just hadn't really noticed or cared. I cared now and I sat up straighter in my chair to scan the lawn. Six out of ten students were vampires. Those were not good odds. A normal statistic should've been one out of ten.

"Why are you asking questions like that?" I glared at the vampire. "If someone was there or not is none of your business. A girl died. You should be considerate."

Of course, he wasn't.

"Hey, hey, I meant no disrespect." The guy held his hands up in mock surrender and made a show of backing up two steps. He grinned charmingly towards me, but I shot out of my seat and leaned closer to him. "A person died that night. I don't care that you're not a person… of virtue. A human being died that night. It makes me wonder why she did. She was *only* human after all… maybe she was pushed into it. Maybe someone who isn't human did it?"

"Davina." Adam stood and touched my shoulder.

I ignored him and held the vampire's gaze steadfast. I wanted to make sure he heard my real meaning. "I know enough about humans and those who like to think they are. I know which category you fit in."

"That's enough, Davina."

"You should go… you and your friends."

The vampire hated it. He caught every nuance of my threat and probably more, but I didn't care. I was trembling so hard. Slowly, too slow for me, he turned and walked away, but he looked over his shoulder and met my gaze. Then he smiled. Damn vampires.

"Davina! What was that? You can't talk to customers like that! He might've joined up as a volunteer."

"Trust me," I muttered underneath my breath. "You don't want him answering that phone."

Adam said something, but I didn't hear it. A figure was weaving lithely through the crowd. Roane. My eyes narrowed when I noticed that he looked like he was on the prowl.

"I'll be right back," I said briefly and pushed off through the crowd.

When Roane stalked his prey, he did it well. I lost him eight times before I finally saw him at the corner of our admissions building. I sprang forward and would've lost him again if I hadn't jumped over two bushes and thrust my way through four groups of students. I stepped on toes and banged against private parts, but I didn't care. I landed with a huff at Roane's feet and bent over gasping. "We need to talk about the Immortal and all of these vampires here."

Roane wrapped a firm hand around my arm and yanked me behind him. I didn't have time to blink before I found myself pushed up against a building wall as Roane glared at me.

"Huh?" I was still focused on breathing.

"You better think long and hard before you start throwing out words like that to me." Roane glared at me with deadly intent.

Oh. Whoa. I blinked as I took in the sight of him again. The shadow from the building hit his face to accentuate his angular cheekbones. His tight shirt molded against his form, highlighting his lean muscles that would've had any A-List actor drooling in envy. Then there was the air surrounding him. He looked capable of killing. He might've been a forceful dick, but I'll admit he was hot. He even smelled of danger. My eyes shifted to see his teeth showing. I knew that his fangs could elongate out from their gums and he could jump nine feet at times. That's how far the other hunters had jumped on Craig. Their fangs had been bared to the flames before they sunk them into his flesh.

"Davy!" He hissed and clamped his other hand to my arm. He had me trapped in place now.

"Wha—huh?"

"What are you talking about?"

I shrugged out of his hold. "Kates told me about your fairytale. Whatever. But there are *way* too many vampires at this convention for it to be a coincidence. What is going on?"

He relaxed slightly—which unnerved me. "They're harmless."

"I don't want them here. This is my world. I go to college here. I'd like all the vampires to just leave!"

He laughed.

He laughed.

The lethal Hunter that scared me the most laughed at me. "Hey!" I hit his shoulder, but vampire bodies are sculpted and hardened to withstand anything. My hand literally bounced off of his shoulder and I was the one that gasped from the pain.

"What?"

I cradled my hand to myself and gritted my teeth when it started to throb. "Don't laugh at me."

"I'm not. Yes, the Immortal is in town. They're here for her. It's like when humans flock to wherever the pope shows up. I can't make them leave so you're going to have to deal with their presence."

"They hurt people."

"That's my problem. Trust me, I can handle my job." Roane turned and gestured towards the hotline booth with his head. "I thought you quit that place."

"What? Huh?" I looked over and sure enough, I could see the booth through a line of pine trees that blocked us from the convention. There he was, hard at work. My Adam. My hero. And he was currently answering some more vampires' questions. His hand didn't tremble. He didn't sweat. He had no idea those things were vampires. I saw how eager he was. He thought he was recruiting future volunteers. Unlike those vampires, his heart was in the right place.

"I saw you over there. I thought you quit."

Roane pulled me back to our conversation. I felt off balance from my Adam daydreams and then Roane's presence was a world in itself. The force that came from him was sweltering and it seemed to suck a person in. I shook my head again and tried to get past a little dizziness.

Oh… no… no. I realized with horror that the dizziness wasn't going anywhere. In fact, the world was starting to circle around me at breakneck speed. I felt myself falling and I shot out a hand for balance. The building in front of me felt sturdy as I leaned my head against it. It was really nice to touch.

And then… double crap. Everything went black.

CHAPTER TWELVE

I found myself in a dark secluded room and on top of an uncomfortable couch when I woke up. Where the hell was I?

"We're in a professor's office."

I jumped abruptly and let out a shriek. Then I saw a shadow detach itself from the wall and stroll forward. Roane.

"You fainted." His voice was curt.

"You caught me before? I thought it was the building."

He leaned back on the desk and asked, "What's going on with you? You were vomiting the other night and I know you weren't drunk. Now you fainted. You look like you've been sick since last night. Cold sweats?"

"Why do you care? It's none of your business. How did you know about the cold sweats?" I didn't think I wanted to hear the answer.

"I can smell the perspiration on your skin."

I'd been right.

"It's got a sweet aged smell to it. Not many vampires can place it."

"Too much information."

"You asked."

"Well, I wish I hadn't now." My voice sounded like I'd just sang the lead in an opera—as a novice.

"Your throat hurts?" Was there sympathy in that voice?

"Yeah." It felt like I'd swallowed bark and then vomited it back up, still fully formed.

Roane crossed and sat in the chair beside my head. He leaned forward on his knees and regarded me intently. Why did the chair have to be positioned so close to the couch? Why did Roane's hands brush slightly against my shoulder and why didn't I suppress the shiver this time? I swallowed tightly and grimaced from the pain. The shivers were becoming normal to me. Somehow, I was certain that wasn't a good thing.

"You might be able to ignore that something's going on with you, but I won't."

I slowly and achingly sat up. "Why do you care?"

"Because I might need you if Kates goes against the decree again. You're still the only person she'll listen to and contrary to what you think; I really don't want to kill your friend."

What every girl wants to hear. "Well… thanks for not wanting to kill my friend." What every girl wants to say.

"Have you talked to anyone about your symptoms?"

"You sound like a counselor or a doctor. It's annoying. And no, I haven't said anything. You know that, it's why you brought me in here from the convention—the convention! Adam! Did you—"

Roane stood and crossed to the window. He peeked through the drawn blinds. "Your boyfriend thinks you had an emergency and that's why you were called away. Don't worry; I had someone pass along the message." Did I detect a slight smirk at the corner of his lips? I could only imagine what that might mean… "Can you stand?"

"Uh… yeah… I mean… can I have a minute here?" I swallowed underneath those impenetrable eyes of his.

"I can help, you know."

I knew instantly what he meant and I felt myself pale. "No, no, no. I am not drinking your blood. I don't care if it'll heal whatever wrong's with me."

"I thought I'd offer."

"Again. No."

Roane stood up. The chair didn't even creak. It looked old, uncomfortable, and pink. I felt the couch creak underneath my weight so I knew that if I'd been the one to stand up from the chair, it would've sounded like a falling tree. Not Roane with his supernatural grace. Not even Kates could move how he did. Something told me that Roane was not the vampire to be pitted against. I shivered at that thought and for once I was thankful the Hunters were on my side.

"You should go home and rest for the night."

I could rest, yes, but not for the night. "I can't. I have a date tonight."

"With your boyfriend?" He said it so calmly and evenly. I frowned when I couldn't discern what he might be thinking—and why the hell did I care about that?

"With Adam. He's taking me to the Alexander Restaurant. It's supposed to be divine eating." I almost tripped on my own self-righteousness.

"I own it." His voice was flat. Emotionless.

"Let me know how that makes sense. I didn't know that vampires were such 'divine' chefs."

"You should stop stereotyping us. You know that we're not all the same, Davy."

I heard the seductive promise and I hated how my body reacted. "Is it hot in here?"

"I'm not Adam either. You like him because you can control him. You don't like me because you can't manipulate me. You can't control me."

"You're not very normal for a vampire either." Had I just admitted to being manipulative?

"Truth hurts. Deal with it." Roane turned back towards the window.

"What's out there? You keep looking out there. Are you looking for something in particular?"

"More like *someone* in particular."

"And that makes sense." Sarcasm.

Whatever Roane was going to say was interrupted as his eye caught and held on something. I saw a slight grin appear and vanish just as quickly, but his eyes remained on whatever spot he watched. He withdrew abruptly from the window and crossed to the office door. It wasn't even a second before he opened it and another giant vampire stepped through. It almost looked coordinated, but who coordinates that? *'Vampires would.'* I snorted at that thought. Roane ignored me, but the other vampire lifted a pair of shrewd dark eyes my way. They were cold. No—scratch that. They were freezing. And they didn't want me there.

"Who is this?" Even his voice sounded like the tundra.

"No one. Did you find something?"

He drew up to his fullest height, which was impressive. I guessed he might've been over six feet and five inches, but I'm terrible at guessing that stuff. With his broad shoulders and his rich golden curls, the vampire could've passed as a member of the royal Viking family. "Raitscliff and Lucan have both found a female that might be the next."

"Their families are here?"

The Viking nodded and waited for Roane's command.

Roane nodded once. His shoulders were made of stone. "Call the rest. I can't fight both families alone."

"You are not alone." The Viking sounded sincere. He laid a gentle hand on Roane's shoulder and I was more surprised when it wasn't shrugged off. Roane seemed to get strength from the simple touch.

"I know I am not alone, Gregory, but I would fear for your life too heavily. Raitscliff has vowed your death since Hartsdale."

"He can try." Gregory puffed up as his hand formed a tight fist.

He had meaty hands. I could only imagine the damage one of those hands could inflict. Just… impressive…and horrifying.

"Find Wren and I'll meet you back at the house."

"And her?" He sneered at me.

I straightened and fixed him with one of my glares. I could do the frostbite thing back at him. I think my glare bounced off him how my hand had bounced off of Roane before.

"Go." Roane ignored Gregory.

Gregory clamped his jaw tight and abruptly disappeared from the room. He didn't literally vanish, but the effect was the same. He was there. He was gone. And the door clicked in his wake.

"Boyfriend?"

Roane ignored me as he moved back to the window and peered through the blinds. Then he heaved a deep unnecessary breath.

"Why do you do that?"

"What?"

"Breathe. Sigh. Why do you do that? You don't actually breathe, you know. You don't need air."

Roane studied me for a moment. "It's habit. It's the body's habit. I try to grant the wish of the body."

"It's not like you're a demon that inhabits it. It was your body before you became a vampire."

He measured his words, but I caught the slightest inflection of… remorse? "To me, I was taught to respect the soul and the vessel of the soul. My mind might be similar, but I am not human, Davy. I don't have that soul anymore. The body misses the soul. It's a unique relationship that can't be described, but there are vestiges. There are little remains that tell me what the body used to do with the soul. Breathing is just one of them."

Well—that was… very philosophical. I wasn't sure I was glad that I had asked. "Oh."

"You're a human, Davy. And yet, you're more than the others. You know of us. You know of our world. You look down on us, but I'm human enough to know that you fear us. You went through a terrible thing with one vampire. I understand that his scars are still in you, that you think and feel because of them. They have power over you and yet—I think you're above those scars. I think you *can* be above them."

I was blown away and infuriated by what he said. I was also pissed, though I wasn't sure why. "You're a Hunter. You're a vampire. You own a restaurant. I'm guessing that you own a few of them. You go to college. Why do you even bother going to classes? Why pretend to be one of the lowly creatures we are?"

Roane took a step forward.

I leaned forward on the edge of the couch.

He studied me like he was absorbing my image into his brain.

I let him. I soaked up the attention—I'm not above admitting that. I wanted that attention. I wanted his attention. And I held my breath...

"Why pretend? That's your question? You shouldn't ask it that way. You shouldn't put us above you. Because it's not like that, Davy. The new decree is supposed to remind us what it's like to be human. Humanity. That's what everything is for us. Some forget. Some want to forget. It's about us not forgetting what we used to be. We used to be human. We used to have that soul inside of us and we cling to anything that will help us keep that reminder." Roane surged forward. "Education is the right for any soul. There is a potential that is only granted freedom through education. To not learn, that's to forget a soul's humaneness."

And that was said by a vampire. "Good thing I'm in college then…"

"Don't joke this off. Don't cover up what you are."

"I…" I opened my mouth, but what was there to say? I didn't know… I couldn't even formulate a thought. I just knew that my heart was pounding like a thundering racetrack.

Roane opened his mouth, but closed it abruptly. He glided forward.

I couldn't think.

He was only an inch away.

I couldn't… his hand swept upwards…

I closed my eyes… his hand cupped the side of my cheek… then I gasped as his lips touched mine.

CHAPTER THIRTEEN

His lips held mine softly, sensually, for a brief moment before his mouth opened over mine. He didn't demand entry, but I gasped and his tongue slid sweetly inside.

My hand held weakly onto his shoulder. Roane slid a hand down my arm to my waist and over my thigh. He lifted me in the air and sat me down on the edge of the desk. As my legs parted, he fit perfectly. A bubble burst inside of me and the remnants coursed through my entire body. I felt the heat fill my fingers, my toes, and even my neck where his thumb caressed lightly.

My body melted, but Roane held me up. As my neck fell backwards, his hand held me still and his lips pressed fluttering kisses down to my throat. His belt buckle rubbed against the inside of my leg and then his hand lifted my leg to dangle it over his. I felt his body stiffen and surge against me. He paused once and I knew what he wanted. Every muscle stood out, prominent, from his skin. I saw the struggle in his stormy eyes. They were always coal black, but there was a silvery haze over them this time. He was hungry.

And then…Roane drew in a ragged breath and I saw the decision jerk through his body. I felt the shudder against me, between my legs, and then I felt cold. Roane moved back and I felt the magic rip out from inside of me. I ached. It was like I was starving and been given something to eat, only to have it taken away after one taste. I wanted more and I reached forward without thinking.

Roane weakly batted away my hand, but I caught his instead and hauled him forward. He was back between my legs, where he was supposed to be. This time I took control. I felt the indecision shudder through his body. My hand slid up his back and over each of his chiseled muscles to his corded neck, then down around his arm. I felt over his chest and explored the dip between each muscle in his stomach.

My eyelids were heavy with desire as I looked up at him, but I didn't know what to say. I felt like I'd been woken to life for the second time. I wasn't about to go back to sleep. With that thought in mind, I drew him closer and met his lips. It was all he needed. Roane took control. His hands wrapped around me and pulled me on top of him.

I wanted the barrier gone, but Roane ripped away from me again to slam a hand over the door. The door tried to open, but Roane barked out something. It sounded unintelligible to my ears, but I saw that the door remained shut after that.

I gasped for breath. Cold air slammed against my insides. Oh god…. Oh… god….

"Turn your shield on."

What? I looked up, but struggled to see Roane. It was like a black veil had fallen over my eyes. I knew he was there. I heard him, but I couldn't see him. Then my body twitched and I drew in a panicked breath. I felt the desk underneath me. It was rattling and I realized, as if I were in the distance, that it was me. I was making the desk shake uncontrollably. I didn't…

"Davy!"

Roane's voice was so far away.

"Roane," I heard myself whimper.

"She's going into shock, Lucas."

That wasn't Roane. I frowned, but I felt myself falling backwards and then something caught me. I knew it was Roane, but I couldn't see him. I opened my mouth to talk to him and ask him who had come into the room, but no sound came out.

"Her heart is going crazy. You have to put her out."

"Shut up, Wren!" Roane snarled.

"Her body is changing, but she's still with us. Put her out, Lucas!

She's scared right now. Put her out and she'll be fine when she wakes up."

I felt Roane's chest jerk upwards, as if he couldn't make the decision. I heard the struggle in his voice. "I… the dreams, Wren. I can't… you don't know what they go through."

"No." The girl was cold. "This girl is not Talia. This girl is the new one and you have to put her out. She has to have those dreams, Lucas. They *all* have to have those dreams. She has to know what she is. Put her out."

I felt the surrender in Roane's arms before he bent over my body. His hand wrapped around my throat and then…

"Welcome." The voice was harsh and sarcastic, but also upbeat.

I looked up and saw nothing. I was in a black hole.

"You know you're dreaming. We know you're dreaming. Everyone knows you're dreaming." The words came again. They rushed at me from behind this time.

I sat up, shaken, but was surprised to find strength surge through my body. I flexed my hand slowly and held it in front of me. My hand wasn't my hand. I saw through my hand, through my skin and my blood. Everything was silver. It ran through my entire body and was pumping into my heart.

Oh my god—Roane! Kates! Anyone!

"Stop whining." It whipped around me again. I heard a laugh this time.

"Who—what are you?"

"This is the circus, didn't you know? We're in Alice's Wonderland with the seven berry gummy bears. Exciting, right? I know you're on the edge of your seat. I would be if I had a seat, but I don't. I'm shapeless. I have no form. I have no solid. I'm the gray in between." The voice bounced around me.

"You're psychotic. That's what you are." I drew in a breath.

"I like you. I didn't like the last one. She was weak."

"Weak?"

"Yeah."

Suddenly, the girl from the roof stood in front of me. She wasn't poised on the edge of the roof, not like that night or in my dream. This time she wore a yellow sweater over white jeans. Her red curls hung loosely down to her waist.

"Her." The voice was disgusted.

"I was there that night."

"She died because you were there. If you hadn't shown up on that roof, she couldn't have died. She could've stabbed herself in the artery and she would've lived through it. But you already knew that, didn't you?"

I closed my eyes, but I saw the same thing. Blackness. I opened my eyes and the girl was gone.

"It's annoying when you do that."

"Do what?" But I didn't want to know. I wished that I would wake up.

"When something happens that you don't like, you try to escape it. You should stop. It's a bad habit. Freaky Cinderella needs to see her toad or she might step wrong and squash him."

"I'm in a psych hospital, right? I'm having hallucinations and I'm actually schizophrenic. That's what you are. You're me talking to me and this doesn't exist."

"Little Jack can't run without his Jill. The pail won't let them."

Yep. I was insane. "I need to go right now. I can pinch myself. I'll wake up. Or I can kill myself. You always wake up before you die, right?"

"There are rules, Jackass." It screamed this time and with a blink of the eye I saw the girl again. She stood in front of me, looking through me, and I saw the hazel eyes from before. They weren't sad or content this time. They were terrified and she quaked beneath my stare. Then someone passed me and I saw that she didn't tremble because of me. She knelt as a black form loomed above her. It was a person, but the shape was too blurry. I couldn't see who it was. I really wanted to know who it was. "Trees stand on the ground. The sun sets and rises again. The moon beams down. Waves roll back and forth and what's underneath it all? Rules."

"Who is that?" I gestured to the black shape. Something was before me and I needed to know what it was. I felt the urgency shoot through my body and I glanced from the corner of my eye to my arm. I screamed as I saw the silver course through all of my body and explode outwards into a blinding light. The black shape was illuminated a man with a scar that ran from his eyebrow down his face to end below his neck. He held a jagged dagger in his hand and blood dripped from the tip.

"Who is that?"

"Would Jack and Jill have run up the hill if they had no pail?"

I felt a poke in my side. "Stop it."

The voice laughed. "That wasn't me, Freaky Cinderella."

"Don't call me Freaky Cinderella," I snarled and whirled around. Nothing. Darkness. As I whirled the other way I saw the same girl, but the scarred man was gone. She held the dagger this time and I watched, frozen, as she took the knife to her arm and gritted her teeth. As sweat beaded over her eyebrows, she started to cut her own skin.

"She was the Freaky Cinderella," the voice whispered in my ear.

"Who are you?"

"The water."

"Who's the pail?"

"You."

Not the answer I was expecting. "And Jack and Jill are...?"

"Wrong answer, Freaky Snow White."

I was Snow White now. "Could you pick one fairy tale and keep with it? I'm getting confused."

"You haven't been kissed yet. The seven berry gummy bears won't let you be kissed. I wouldn't like them if I were you."

"Thank goodness that you're not me then," I snapped back.

There was a pause. I felt surprise in the air. "The seven berry gummy bears need to die."

"I'll eat them. How about that?" I was nearing the end of my rope. The voice was starting to irritate me. I liked gummy bears and I hated fairy tales. "Reveal yourself. Now." I felt the resistance in the air. It swirled around me. As I pulled one way, it pulled the other way. Then I screamed, "Reveal!"

The air exploded. I blinked from the force of it and then I saw myself staring back at me. The real me was annoyed. "Who are you?"

"The water."

Oh yes. I was a sarcastic brat. "No riddles. Who are you and who am I?"

The other me smirked. "I'm the water. You're the pail, but you need to figure out who Jack and Jill are."

"Humans and vampires."

"Try something more elemental than that. Those are species. Look at yourself."

I glanced down to my arms and lifted them high. I still saw the silver color pumping through my skin. I saw the tendons and ligaments attached to my muscles and bones. The silver ran through it all. I was a little unnerved, but I gritted my teeth. There had to be a message in all this nonsense.

"You're life."

"I'm Davy."

"That's what we can call you, but that's not what you are. Not anymore."

"I'm…" I looked up, somber. "Jack and Jill don't exist. You're the Immortal. You're life and you're in me now. It's not about Jack and Jill. It's about running up the hill and falling down. It's about fetching the pail. They wouldn't have to run up the hill if they didn't need to fetch a pail of water."

"You're starting to get it. She never got it."

"The hill is…"

"The hill is the pursuit. You're the golden prize."

I was going to wake up. I felt it slowly coming…. My other self disappeared in a flash, but the voice haunted me, "You're the Immortal now, Davy. Welcome to the Land of Never Death."

Then I gasped as the dagger flashed towards me. Blood dripped down and it was mine this time. The dagger swept closer and embedded itself in my chest. I opened my mouth to scream, but no sound came out.

CHAPTER FOURTEEN

My eyes snapped open and I let loose a shrill scream. My hand clamped on my chest, but it took a moment before I realized that there was no dagger. There was no blood. My hand shook as I held it out and saw there that was no silver blood. My hand was normal. Pale. I looked around and there was no Alice's Wonderland. I breathed a sigh of relief.

"You're awake."

I turned towards the voice and was dazed to see a hooker leaning against a grand oak door. She wasn't really a hooker, but she looked like one. She smiled coolly and straightened from her post, then stalked towards me with one precisely placed black boot in front of the other. She was a vampire. That was obvious, but she wasn't like the other vampires around Benshire. They dressed like regular folk. She wore a black leather corset held together by silver safety pins. The leather looked like it cut into her skin, but I doubted she cared. It's not like she really needed to breathe. It gave her some massive cleavage.

The corset looked like it was tucked into her pants. The ends were tucked inside those high-heeled black boots that started below her knees.

Uncomfortable. Dangerous. Sexy.

Her dark eyes flickered and I almost expected to see a drop of blood at the corner of her mouth. It would've blended with her lipstick and the auburn curls that hung down to her waist.

"So… welcome back." She clipped those words out.

"You say that, but I don't think your heart's really into it," I replied with a raspy voice. I frowned and glanced down—that's when I saw where I was. Black satin sheets. I was in a massive bed placed on a pedestal in the center of the room. The bed was… whoa. That's all I could say and the rest of the room…. I took a second look at the doors since they were my only exit. They were massive too and made of oak with little swirls in the frame around the doors, like an artist had custom-made the frames just for the room. The swirls in the frame matched the two window frames, bed posts, and headboard. Someone was more decorative than me. Then I looked at myself and saw I was dressed in my jeans with only my thin camisole. That was it. No socks. I always wore socks. I loved my socks. "Where am I?"

"Lucas wanted to make sure you were safe."

"What happened to me?"

Her body is changing… My body shook as I remembered those words and I focused on her again. "You know who I am? You were there. You said—" I fell silent, confused. How had she known? I hadn't even known.

She was smug. "Do I know who you are? Yes. I'm one of three who knows. And yes, I was there when your body started changing. You were seizing. I had to put you out of your misery."

I sat further up in the bed. "You told Roane to do it. You told him that I needed 'to know.'" My throat was sore so I started to massage it.

"Now you know… don't you?" I saw a flash of dislike in her eyes and knew this vampire *really* loathed me.

I threw my legs out from underneath the sheets and stood weakly.

"He's not going to want you to leave. Lucas said to keep you here no matter what." There was a warning in her dark eyes. So I made sure there was a wide berth as I rounded to the door. When I reached it, I held her gaze. That's when I saw that she had no intention of stopping me. Why? Did she really hate me that much? Was it about Roane?

As those questions formed in my mind, I was inside her. Her shields were like air for me. She had no idea. She was frozen in place, like I had paralyzed her. I could easily slip through now whereas I would've broken a sweat before.

"No, Davy." A hand wrapped around my arm and jerked me out.

So many things flashed through my mind, but I watched as she blinked. She was slowly coming out of her trance. Then comprehension flashed and loathing quickly followed. It had been there before, but this time it was tenfold and she bared her fangs. If Roane hadn't been there, she would've killed me.

Roane pulled me against his chest and tucked me to the side at the same time. He moved and stood between the two of us. "Wren, walk away. She doesn't know her powers yet. Go."

Wren straightened to her full height. She didn't spare Roane a glance, but she promised so many lethal things in her eyes. If Wren had been at Kates' bar, I knew I would've tucked tail and just left Emily to fend for herself. Not now. I felt something in my gut. I held a hand over my stomach and the feeling instantly speared to my skin, like I had called it there. It on the other side of my skin and I watched horrified and amazed as a spark came out of it. "Oh my god!"

"She's going into shock again. She can't handle it." Take a guess at who said that.

"Not now, Wren," Roane snarled as he swept his arms underneath me and I felt myself being lifted in the air.

"Put her out again. She can't handle it, not yet. It's too soon. Her body changed too fast, Lucas. Put her out."

"No!" I struggled in Roane's arms, but he laid me on the bed and held me down.

"Calm down, Davy. You have to calm down. I know it's hard. I know the adjustment is disconcerting, but please stay with me."

"She can't handle it. She'll be another kicker before the week's end."

"Out!" Roane roared this time.

I slammed back into reality and felt Roane's body on top of mine. I heard his ferocity. He was tense and hard like a rock, but his attention was focused on her.

My palm itched. I looked at it, detached from myself, and saw it jerk. It was like it knew I watched it, like it had something it wanted to do. I wasn't sure what was going to happen, but I knew something was going to happen. It closed on itself and I felt a searing heat flare through my body. My hand trembled, but it remained fisted and then the heat surged through my body again and soared to my hand. The heat burst out of my body and shot through the air. It aimed perfectly.

Wren saw it coming. The heat slammed against her chest and she crashed backwards through the doors. She was there. She was gone.

"Where did you send her?" Roane scrambled off the bed and looked through the opened doors.

"I wanted her gone." We still hadn't heard her fall.

"Gregory!"

"She's okay. She landed in the lilies." Gregory's voice echoed through the house.

Roane swung his impenetrable eyes my way from the doorway. "Wren hates lilies. Did you know that?"

My eyes went wide as I realized that when I'd been inside of her, I'd done a quick scan. It was like I was some ultra-charged empath now and I was the internet inside of humans, well, vampires.   I shrugged. "Lucky guess. She didn't look like the flower type."

Roane studied me intently. The silence stretched out. One second. Five seconds. Thirty—a minute—five minutes. Ten minutes. That's how long we stared at each other. Ten freaking minutes. Then, "You don't even need a shield anymore."

"That's all? I heat-rayed your girlfriend out of this house. All you say is that I don't need a shield anymore?"

Roane didn't change expressions. "You're changing, Davy. You know that you're changing and you know what you're changing into. Talia needed a shield and you don't. It's… remarkable."

I didn't like that name. In fact, I loathed that name. "Who is Talia?"

"She was the Immortal before you."

"I know that look," Roane announced a few hours later as he strode back into the room and closed the doors behind him. I knew he'd left to deal with Wren, but I didn't care to ask what had happened. She was gone. I was glad and then I thought better of it when I watched him close those doors. It might've been his slow movements or how he paused before he pulled those two doors shut, but the entire movement was ominous.

I sat up slowly and swallowed tightly. My hands fisted into the satin sheets, but it was all I could do. I was afraid to move. I was afraid to breathe. I was even afraid to think. He looked long and hard as if to see inside of me. He might've been. He knew more about me than I did.

"What look?" I wasn't sure I wanted to hear his answer.

Roane gestured with a nod. "You don't want to be here. Are you thinking of your little human boy? Are you hoping that he'll take you away from here? You want to forget everything that's happened this last week?"

He had no idea… how right he was. "Just because you can read other people's thoughts doesn't mean that you can read mine."

"I can't anymore, but I could before. Now there's no way to get into that head. She wasn't like that."

'She.' Something about that word did not sit well with me. I didn't want him to know, though, so my voice didn't tremble when I asked, "She? Talia?"

Roane did his thing again. He measured me up and down for thirty seconds. "Yes. She was a good person."

"She wasn't really a person, was she?"

"You're right. She wasn't really a person."

"Even though that's what the lore says about Immortals. That they're human, but they have immortality."

"They?"

"I'm the last in a long line, right? Wren said that I'm not going to make the week before I'm on that rooftop."

Roane took one of those habitual small breaths and leaned against the wall. He was across the room and yet, I felt suffocated by his presence. He was too close. He wasn't close enough. I was on his bed. I wasn't in his arms. I sucked in a harsh breath and shook my head. I couldn't think like that—I couldn't feel like that. It was wrong. Everything was wrong.

"I understand it, you know." He sounded raw, scraped open.

Something relaxed inside of me. I didn't feel so alone. "Understand?"

He moved closer. I didn't see it, but I sensed it. I felt him move beside the bed, but he didn't sit down. He stayed beside me, but just out of reach.

"You're going through it again. You were empathic. You couldn't control your gifts. I heard you with Kates, how horrible it must've been. I'm a vampire, Davy. I understand the complexities between Empaths and Vampires. I know you must've been tortured."

'Hey, little girl, little girl, little girl. Come out and play... come out and play. I have some toys for you.'

"Do you really?" I strangled out. "Do you know what he did to me? The things that he said and that was just... those were words. They weren't even... do you really understand what he did to me?"

I looked up and was caught by Roane's gaze. In the span of knowing him, he was usually so unemotional. There were times that I knew I'd infuriated him. There were times I'd been intimidated by him. I'd felt what it was like to be inside his arms, but I'd never seen this from him.

He was haunted.

"Were you tortured?" I don't know why I asked.

"I did the torture, Davy."

'It's about us not forgetting what we used to be. We used to be human.'

"That must've been…." I wasn't sure what to say. That must've been *hard* for him? He did the torture and I'd been tortured. I was suddenly angry, really angry at him even though he hadn't been my torturer. Not to mention that I wasn't human anymore. Would I turn into the same monster?

"That's not…" Roane stopped and turned away, but paused before he had completely turned his back. He raised a hand and ran it over his head.

I drew my knees to my chest and hugged them. I could see he was upset, but so was I. "I'm not human anymore, Roane. You can't—" He couldn't understand. He'd been a vampire for so long.

"What? I can't understand? I have no idea what it's like to suddenly wake up and not be human, with powers that don't make sense. You're right, Davy. I have absolutely no idea."

I shrunk back from his stinging words.

Roane pressed, "I know more about you than you do right now, Davy. I know what the Immortal is. I know that you're empathic and you're still human. You've just got other juices flowing in your blood."

"Can I get rid of them?" I kneeled on his bed. A part of me was desperate. I didn't want this.

Roane sucked in his breath, but didn't move away. He didn't move closer either, but he couldn't look away. I felt my power over him. It was blinding and I knew that he couldn't turn away. He wanted to. A part of him really wanted to turn and walk away. He didn't.

I moved closer, just close enough without touching him. If either of us moved an inch, we would've felt the other.... I wanted to feel him. I needed it. It was the same hunger that I'd felt in that professor's office. Something inside of me—or maybe it was me—needed him. It was like I was starving for him.

Roane searched my face, but his eyes flickered and held on my lips. He wrung out, "You don't know yourself right now. This isn't what you want."

"This isn't what happened in the office? That was both of us."

"You were starting to change. You weren't yourself. You won't be, not for a long time."

"Are you trying to save me, Roane? Is that what this is? You're trying to be compassionate? Maybe feeling your human self right now?"

I felt the whiplash from his eyes. He was furious, but he clenched his jaw tight. "You don't want me to save you or you don't want to be saved? You want me to be a vampire, Davy? Is that what you want? Maybe you want me to drink your blood? Davina."

Davina.

Vampire.

I lifted stormy eyes to his. "You have this decree to stop yourselves from being what you are. It's the same thing as Kates. She's meant to be a slayer and that decree says she can't be herself. You're evil. Be evil and she can do what she's supposed to do. She gets to kill you."

His lip curled upwards, mocking and lethal. "And that's what pisses you off, because you don't know where you fit in. You've never known, have you? You're a human. You're not supposed to know about us, but you do. You're empathic and that made you a freak. You found out things you weren't supposed to and now what are you? You're more of a freak than Kates or I will ever be. Only one can exist and you're all alone."

Those words hit me, but he was right. "I am alone and I don't know who I am—what I am."

"Davy…"

"Kates said that you want my blood? I have life in me and you want that life?" Everything was blaring inside of me. "You…"

"It's not that simple."

"Then make it simple!" I cried out, infuriated. There was something inside of me, something that I didn't understand. I wanted it out. I wanted it gone because it didn't belong there. It wasn't me and I only wanted to be me. "I don't want this, Roane! I don't want this thing inside of me. Take it out. Drink it out. Drain me—do whatever you need to do. I want it gone!"

'Welcome to the Land of Never Death.'

"Get it out of me!" I grasped Roane's shoulders and pressed myself against him. I felt him stiffen. He was so rigid…. "Please, Roane."

He sighed in surrender and wrapped both arms around me.

Just then, we heard a cough and I nearly wept, but I couldn't name from what emotion. Roane lifted his head and I felt the coldness where he had rested his cheek against mine. He turned towards the intruder. "What is it, Gregory?"

"The Family is here. They need to know about her."

Her—me. I felt the reluctance in Roane and though he didn't move I still felt a part of him tear away from me. I almost gasped from the pain. "They can't know, Gregory. No one can know." It was like he'd spoken about death, about his death.

"Raitscliff and Lucan both think the new Immortal is a different girl."

"Do you know this girl?"

"Yes."

"Then go and get her. They can't hurt her if we have her."

"You'll bring war to this household," Gregory warned.

I glanced towards the Viking vampire and was surprised to see the gravity in his eyes.

Roane wrapped his arms tighter around me. I closed my eyes as his cheek brushed against mine and felt his words against my shoulder. "Find the other girl. Bring her here."

When Gregory left, I looked up. "What'll happen to the other girl?"

Something broke inside of Roane at my question. A part of me realized that I was in there because I felt it break. I hadn't purposely gone into him, but I was. He either didn't care or didn't know. "They'll drain her. They'll kill her thinking she can't die. But even if she was the Immortal, I would still need to stop them."

"Why?"

"No vampire can drink the Immortal's blood. It can't be allowed to happen."

I lifted my head and searched his eyes with mine. *'How?'*

"I'll fight them."

I pulled away and out of him at the same time. Everything was too much. "This is all too overwhelming."

"It's going to get more overwhelming."

"What do you mean?"

"You should sit down, Davy."

That didn't sound ominous at all. "Okay…" I sat slowly and took a breath. I knew I'd need to ready myself for whatever was coming my way.

He stepped back and leaned against the wall "In all my life, no Immortal has been known."

CHAPTER FIFTEEN

"What do you mean? You knew the other girl. You said she was a good person."

"I did know her, but I was the only one, Davy. I knew Talia when she was little and I protected her. That was my job. I wasn't always a Hunter. I became one because… certain Elders questioned me…"

I straightened. "You're not telling me everything."

"No, I'm not. That's not important at this time. You need to know about the Immortal and you need to understand the situation. You're the new Immortal. I suspected before, but I wasn't sure."

"Why do the other vampires think it's someone else? I was on that roof with Talia. They saw me."

"But they didn't see her touch you. There was no contact between you two."

'*Yeah, but… I felt inside of her.*'

Roane read my thoughts. "The Immortal thread goes from one human to the next. She didn't touch you. They don't know about the psychic contact between you. No one else knew about that possibility. It's always been documented in the Immortal lore that one Immortal needs to physically touch the next Immortal. *I* knew that it didn't need to happen that way, but no one else knew."

"She touched someone else?"

Roane nodded. "Another girl left the building when Talia went inside. Talia held the door open for her and their arms brushed against each other."

"But…" Too many questions. Not enough answers. "What did you mean when you said that no Immortal has been known?"

"You said before that the Immortal was a fairytale and you're somewhat right. There's always been the belief that an Immortal existed, but no one knew for certain. There were theories, but Talia was hidden by my family. I was entrusted to protect her, but I failed."

I felt how his words hurt him. This was his duty. It's what I felt inside of him the first time we spoke. "You were supposed to protect her and hide her?"

Roane nodded, his jaw tight.

"What happened? How'd the other vampires find out?"

Something told me that Roane wasn't going to share the details unless he absolutely had to. "I'd been sent on a different mission for one of the Elders so I wasn't even there. But there was an argument and the wrong person overheard. Talia made a choice—she ran that night. She knew she needed to find another Immortal and hoped the Immortal would remain hidden. She did what she needed to do."

"She chose me?" He still wasn't telling me everything.

"The Immortal thread chose you, not Talia. You were supposed to work late that night. She knew you'd come upstairs and she knew you were empathic. She needed to let go of the thread without them seeing it. When you went inside of her, the thread came back with you."

"We aren't supposed to touch too deep in a person." I wet my dry lips. They felt like they were bleeding. "If something went wrong, a part of us could stay inside. I never thought that a part of them could come inside of me. That's not how it's supposed to happen. There are rules, universal laws of nature stuff and…"

"The Immortals can bend those rules."

That meant… "I can bend those rules."

"You can't think that way, not yet. You don't know all of your powers and we don't have time for you to get acquainted with them." Roane surged forward. "That's why I'm giving you this crash course. Gregory's right. I *am* bringing war to this household, but I have to keep you hidden. No vampire can drink from you. If they did, they would have your powers. Any vampire would be unstoppable. I can't let that happen."

I'm back to my dislike for vampires. Evil creatures, the lot of them… well… the possible exception might be in front of me. "Let me guess… when that happens then the world might end?"

"Hardly. It just means that vampire has too much power. No creature should have that power."

"Except a human."

"Except someone with a soul. Yes."

We're back to that conversation. Souls, humanity, forgetting or not forgetting what it's like to be human. It was all connected. I jerked my head up and down and hoped it resembled a nod. I wasn't holding my breath. "What now?"

Roane paused for a second. It was one of those seconds where you felt your heart was going to explode. "You have to walk away from me and be normal."

"What did you say?" My heart skipped a beat.

Roane stepped towards me, but stopped abruptly. It was like he wanted to come closer, but didn't dare. I completely understood and found myself swaying towards him, but I forced myself to stay on the bed….

"I'm the Hunter here. They know that they can't drink from a human, even if they think she's the Immortal. I have to stop them. They won't think twice when they see the girl here, but they'll start to wonder if you're here too. I know some of these vampires. Each of us has a Family and some Families are more powerful than others. Some extremely powerful Families are coming here and all of them want the Immortal. I can't worry that they'll discover who you are if you're here. You need to go. You need to hide and you can do that by being normal. Don't use your powers. They can't sense your power."

"What about… where's your Family?"

"They're coming."

He was being vague and I didn't like that. My eyes sharpened. "Gregory said war. He wasn't exaggerating."

"He wasn't." Roane looked away and rubbed a tired hand over his jaw. My hand itched to cover his.

"I came here to be normal. I wanted to go to college because that's the normal thing to do. Kates didn't understand it, but she's not like me. She likes being unique or abnormal. She doesn't understand… I wish she did sometimes." I looked up and held his gaze. It was alluring, seductive, but I saw the anger that was repressed. It simmered under the surface. "I have a date tonight. I should go on that date, huh?"

He clenched his jaw for the briefest of seconds. "It would be the 'normal' thing to do, yes."

I wondered if it cost him to say that. It cost me to hear it. "Okay. I'll… I'll go on that date, then."

Roane stayed where he was.

I couldn't bring myself to walk out those doors. "I… I should go."

He nodded again. "Gregory will be back with the girl shortly. Hopefully, after awhile, things will go back to normal. You should… stay away from Kates. Stay with your roommate, with that boy. Go to classes. Do your normal thing."

I frowned as a thought came to me. "You said that you needed me to help Kates. Did you? Or was that whole thing just a lie because you thought I was the Immortal?"

'Did he use my roommate?'

"I used them both, yes." Roane read my mind again.

I thought my shields were up against him? "And my powers? What if…"

"Try not to get angry. Talia told me that she used to 'pack it away'. She said some days she was human and the others, she was the Immortal. You could try that."

"What about the other girl? What are you going to do with her?"

Roane answered swiftly and I caught a glimpse of the Hunter he was. I had felt how fierce he could be, how determined and devoted to his duty he was when I'd been inside of him. I had marveled at his motivation and I saw it again when he replied, "We'll hide her. When they demand to know where she is, we'll fight. We'll win. And then she'll be seen in another state, another city, and rumors will be told again. They'll all go there."

They'd leave Benshire and the real Immortal behind. It was brilliant, but something told me that was just Roane doing his job. It was another day in the office for him.

"This is what you do, isn't it." I glided across the room until I stood right before him, within touching distance.

Roane closed his eyes and struggled not to reach out. The same battle was within me… a part of me was starting not to care about the consequences. A part of me was starting to wonder what those consequences actually were. Were there consequences?

Roane caught my hand. I hadn't been aware of lifting it, but he caught and held it immobile in the air. There it was—the connection between us, again. Both of us looked at our hands. His hand wrapped around my wrist. Slowly, hypnotically, I bent my fingers and caressed his finger, just slightly, but it was enough. Roane drew in a ragged breath. I held my own. Then he growled as he hauled me to his chest and lifted me in the air. I wrapped my legs around his waist and we fell on the bed. His weight pressed me down and I searched for his mouth, desperately.

He found it and claimed me.

Roane slid his hands down to my waist. I arched my back to press against him and wrapped my arms around his neck. It seemed like I couldn't get any closer, but I needed to.

I couldn't get enough of him.

And then a phone ring peeled through the air. I cursed under my breath as Roane ripped himself away from me. Instantly, I felt the cold blast against my body and I would've done anything to have him back. The phone rang again and Roane paused when he found it. A third time. "It's… I can't answer this." Roane sounded like he had one last nerve of willpower and the phone was quickly eating it away.

I lifted my head and saw that he had my phone. I'd completely forgotten that I *had* a phone. It seemed like something from a different world, not a world where vampires and Immortals existed.

It rang a fourth time and I felt the impatience across the line. "It's my roommate." I held out a heavy hand and snapped it open. "What?"

"What? You just say it like that? What? Your boyfriend is here. He said something about a date. And you ditched out on the convention today. Thanks a lot. Mr. Moser trusted me and I was stupid enough to trust *you*."

"Emily…"

"Get back here from wherever you are and deal with Adam. I don't want him here."

I sighed in surrender. "I'll be right there."

"Thank you. I'm going to make Adam wait in the lobby for you."

Before I could reply, she'd already hung up.

Roane peered out the window and then looked back. "Gregory's back. I'll have him take you to your dorm."

I wondered if my exhaustion was from the Immortal's change in my body or knowing my life wouldn't be the same again. A third option was the desire that literally throbbed inside of me. My guess—the Immortal had nothing on Roane. When I started towards the door, he stopped me. "Stay away from Wren. Make sure you're never alone with her."

"Why?"

"There are some things that you don't know about her and she knows about you. Avoid her if you see her."

I nodded and left with a heavy heart.

CHAPTER SIXTEEN

"We have seven different types of chairs in the room. Why do we have seven different chairs? It's insane. It's a complete lack of chair-efficiency. I can't handle all these chairs."

This is what greeted me as I stepped inside my dorm room.

Emily was frantic. She had placed every chair in a line, which wasn't long because our dorm room wasn't big. Now she paced with frantic hands in the air.

I frowned and shut the door. "What's going on?"

"He called! Can you believe it? He called. He's downstairs. Right now!"

"Who?"

"That guy from the bar. The one that…" It was endearing how my roommate hung her head and blushed. "…I made out with. I've never done that, Davy." Her eyes were wide and horrified. "I can't believe I did that and now he found me. He's downstairs."

I wasn't sure what my role was here, but I improvised. "What does he want?"

"Dinner," she blurted out.

Horrifying. A slow smile started to spread on my face. "Dinner?"

"Can you believe it? He wants to sit and eat and talk. I don't know what to do."

"Apparently you're categorizing our chairs." I frowned as I looked over the room. There *was* an inordinate amount of chairs. Both of us had desk chairs. There was a pink bean bag that sat beside an inflated purple bean bag. Not to mention the couch, plus another lawn chair—I wasn't sure where that came from. Then there were our regular desk chairs that came with the dorm room. She was right. I counted seven.

"I still feel like crap. Why do I feel like this? I hate being sick. I have too much work to do." Emily moaned and fell into one of the chairs.

A thought occurred to me. "You can come with me and Adam."

Disgust first flashed over her features, but then a bright smile lit it up. "You're right. It's not awkward then. I won't even have to talk. You like to talk. You and Adam can talk, but no mushy stuff. I don't think I can stomach that tonight." She pressed an open palm over her stomach and I feared she was going to *actually* throw up.

I remembered my night of vomiting and grimaced. My stupid body had been changing and I felt a tingle in my palm. My body was *still* changing.

When I turned towards the closet, I muttered to myself, "I don't know if I could stomach it either."

"What's he wearing?"

"Who?"

"The guy!"

"I didn't go through the lounge. I snuck up the back stairs." I shrugged and grabbed my shower bag. Then I toed off my shoes and slid on my flip flops.

"Where are you going?" Emily gasped with a hitch in her voice.

"I'm going to take a shower and then get ready. Adam can wait."

"What about the guy?"

"He can wait too. We're worth it." Then I proved how overjoyed I was with a long yawn.

Emily narrowed her eyes, but didn't comment.

Was I overjoyed? Not anymore. *Could* I be overjoyed with the idea of a date with Adam? I was hoping. I wanted normalcy before and I still wanted normalcy. What was messing it all up was Roane and the Immortal stuff. I shook my head to clear my thoughts. I was a human now. I'd be the Immortal another day. Human. Date. But first, a shower.

When I entered the room after a quick cleaning, I saw that the chairs all remained the same and Emily was dressed now in a pair of khakis and a red sweater. I considered making a joke about Target, but thought better of it. In her state, Emily wouldn't register the joke or she would've been even more horrified.

"I'm freaking out," Emily rushed out.

"Yes. Yes, you are." I nodded to myself.

"What kind of guy comes to a girl's dorm? How did he even know who I was?"

I had one answer for that. He was a vampire. They could sniff down their adversary. "I'm pretty sure Kates introduced you guys or Roane did. It's not that big of a campus. There are only a few dorms for freshman girls."

"Roane?" Emily asked, confused.

"Oh—Luke, right? That's what you call him."

Emily sighed wistfully, "I wish he were downstairs."

My hand stilled as I reached for a black lacy shirt. My stomach flipped on itself, but I took a deep breath and pushed past the moment of shame. My roommate had a crush on Lucas Roane. I knew that and I still kissed him. Could I take it back? I don't think that was the question I needed to ask myself. I should've asked—did I want to take it back?

"But he's not and this guy is. I like this guy—he's… I don't know how to explain it."

I'd heard it so many other times. Emily wasn't the first to have fallen underneath a vampire's attraction. It was ensnaring and powerful. We were both doomed.

"Okay, I'm ready!" Emily announced and I turned to see that she was glowing.

"What happened to the 'we have too many chairs?'"

She blushed again. "I don't know. It's silly, right? I should be excited that a guy is here. He took the time to find me and wants to have dinner. It's dinner. That means something, right? Right?" The glow quickly slipped to show befuddlement.

"It means something, yes."

She smiled and her panic lessened again. I'd never seen her so frazzled. It was so *human* of her and I found that refreshing. "Are you ready to make him eat his heart out?"

Emily smoothed a shaking hand down her shirt and chuckled.

I grabbed my purse and posed. "How do I look?"

Emily blinked. "You look great. Wow, you really do."

I chose a cream silk shirt that hugged my body. A layer of black lace had been sewn over it and the shirt rested low on my hips where I felt the snug fit of my jeans. I had eyed the high heeled black boots, but the black ballet slipper shoes won. I felt comfortable. I knew I wouldn't be mistaken for a Target employee.

As we left the room, I tried not to ask myself the question of whether I was dressing for Adam or the hope of Adam? I sucked in a breath. I didn't want that—I didn't want to start thinking about things like that. I was normal for the night.

Emily had walked ahead, but turned back. Her eyes widened dramatically and she stopped abruptly to place a soothing hand over my arm. "Are you okay?"

"I'm good. Thanks." I was a taken aback at the concern in her voice. It was real. I always thought Emily ran in the opposite direction of emotion. I squeezed her hand in reassurance and then we both turned towards the boys who were waiting. Adam straightened from the wall and smiled that adorable grin.

I felt a calming breath go through me and remembered the reasons why I had liked Adam in the first place. He was sweet and kind. He wasn't evil. There was no hidden agenda.

"You look great, Davina."

"It's Davy." Emily clarified, "She likes to be called Davy."

Score one in the friendship category for my roommate—and from the looks of her leering vampire, she scored a point with him. Unlike Adam's golden curls, this vampire's blond locks looked greasy. Some went for that dirty sex-craved look, but I was glad this one wasn't there for me.

"Emily." The vampire moved from across the room and took her hand gently to rub against his black tight-fitting shirt.

Emily blushed. "Oh my."

"You look beautiful," he crooned as he pulled her towards him and placed a hand around her waist. Well well well… Emily had more than a devoted vampire on her hands.

I eyed him questioningly and wondered if I should slip inside. Then I remembered Roane's words. I was human with human traits and that meant no powers, not even my empathic ones.

"Are you ready to go, Davy?" Adam emphasized my name this time.

"I am and you look good too." And he did, wearing a white pressed shirt over a pair of dark blue jeans.

Emily squeaked when the vampire bent his head and whispered something in her ear. Whatever he said produced another blush and she sounded breathless. "We're going with them."

"We are?" The vampire lazily lifted his head and smiled charmingly.

"We are."

Adam coughed to cover up his surprise. "We're going to the Alexander Restaurant."

"I heard that's divine eating." The vampire was smooth. I had to give him that.

"I don't know if you remember Davy, but this is my roommate. Davy, this is Bennett. He was at that bar we went to with Kates."

"It's nice to meet you this time." I made sure to be polite, but Bennett had no interest in me.

When we got to the cars, Emily insisted all of us go together. As we started off, I sat in the front passenger seat and moved the mirror so I could watch Bennett. I started to realize that something about the vampire bothered me. Of course, it might've been the fact that he was a vampire, but there was something else. He had his hands all over Emily—which I wasn't surprised she allowed. Vampire charm meant vampire addiction. Not many girls could fight the lure once bitten. I knew Emily had no chance so I was secretly happy about the driving status. I could keep an eye on Bennett and make sure he didn't sneak anymore lovebites against Emily's wishes.

Then as we neared the restaurant, I caught some furtive glances that Bennett kept shooting towards Adam. His hands were on Emily, but his eyes were on Adam. What the—? "Bennett, did you and Adam know each other before?"

Bennett lifted his eyes to stare long and hard at me through the rear view mirror. Adam had a look of confusion. He had no clue. So that meant the vampire was up to something. I switched my gaze back to Bennett's in the mirror and wasn't surprised to see him reassessing me.

"Did you guys?" Emily rasped out. "I guess we never introduced you two."

Adam looked like the idea had never occurred to him.

Bennett lied, "We have a class together."

"We do?"

"Yeah. Social work."

"Oh, yeah. The class with Moser?" Adam played into Bennett's hand.

"That's great!" This new Emily was easily satisfied.

I wasn't, but I quieted when Adam pulled into the parking lot. As we got out of the car, I found myself alone with Bennett. Somehow, in the blink of an eye, Emily and Adam had approached the restaurant without us.

"Wha…?" I managed out before Bennett stepped right in front of me.

"You know who I am." He tried to pierce me with his blue eyes. They reminded me of Kates, how fierce and crystal blue they could be at times….

I recovered quickly and snapped out, "I know *what* you are."

"If you're smart, you'll keep that to yourself," he threatened.

"I'm not smart. A lot of people think I'm dumb, really dumb, bimbo dumb." I backed down quickly when I remembered Roane's warning. Loathing vampires drew attention and it certainly wasn't normal. They were used to being feared.

He ran an aggravated hand through his greasy hair. "What do you want?"

"Stop taking lovebites out of my roommate." How many times does a person get to say that?

"Fine. You won't say anything to her? She doesn't know what I am. I'd like to keep it that way."

"You had to have realized that I'd know what you are. Kates was at the bar that night." I knew every vampire knew who and what Kates was.

"What?"

"Kates. She's one of my best friends. She's a slayer, remember?"

"Oh yeah… I never thought… Kates is one of us. She's loyal to Lu—there's a lot of humans that know our secrets and a lot that don't. I'd like Emily to be one that doesn't know."

Whatever he'd been about to say, I wasn't sure I wanted to hear it. By the look of his sudden nervousness and quick catch, I knew Bennett wished that he hadn't slipped what he had.

I stepped closer. "She's loyal to who?"

"Lucas Roane. The Hunter. She's loyal to him like everyone else."

I knew that was a load of crap. He hadn't been about to say Lucas. "She's loyal to him, huh?" I told myself to let it go. My insides screamed that this vampire was bad news, but I was a human that night. Roane made me promise. I couldn't do anything, absolutely anything, to give any suspicion. So that meant I needed to accept that Bennett had lied through his fangs to me.

"She is and so am I. There's no problem, right? I won't hurt your roommate. If I do, I'd have to be killed, remember?"

Right. The whole decree thing… and yet, as he turned and left me behind my gut didn't agree with him.

CHAPTER SEVENTEEN

"I wasn't sure where you went." Adam pulled my chair out for me.

"Uh… yeah…" I didn't think I could tell him a vampire had threatened me.

Adam frowned, but sat beside me as Bennett arrived behind me. There we were. Two couples based on lies and supernatural coincidences. As I looked around, I realized that we were at the best table. The restaurant was nice and by nice—I meant expensive. A fountain was in the middle of the restaurant and each table had a crystal goblet with three small goldfish swimming inside. Our glasses were diamond encrusted.

"Did you request this table?" I asked Adam.

"What?"

"This is the best table in the restaurant. Did you ask for this?"

Bennett lifted his whispering head. Emily fanned herself.

"No. I mean, I called and asked for the availability tonight. They weren't doing reservations. We just got here. I couldn't have… what was the question?"

"Nothing." I shook my head with an easy smile. It didn't matter, but I wondered if Roane had anything to do with the table. I hoped not. It didn't help my confused emotions.

"Shall we order?" Bennett suggested.

I fixed him with a glare. "Right. You're a big fan of… what? Salad?"

"Davy." Both Emily and Adam reprimanded me.

I was nonplussed. "Maybe you can order the meat rare. You can tell them not to cook it, just slap it on a plate for you."

"Davina." Emily had remembered her prim and proper standards. She looked nauseous.

I arched an eyebrow, ready for whatever Bennett threw back, but Adam caught my hand and dragged me from the table.

"What is going on with you?" Adam tried to be nice, but he still sounded aggravated. It was somewhat endearing. He was like a gentleman that needed to ask something ungentlemanly, but couldn't figure out the words.

"I don't like him."

Adam sighed and scratched the back of his head. A surge of warmth speared through me. He really was unlike everything else in my life. Stable. Honest.

"Hey." I caught his hand and pulled it between us. "I like you."

He was startled, but delight spread over his features. "Really?"

I squeezed his hand and moved closer. "I know that it's sudden and fast and this is our first date, but… I just wanted to tell you that. I like you."

"I like you too." An anchor seemed to have lifted off him. "Wow. That feels good to have that off my chest."

This is what I wanted, right? I wasn't sure, but I held tight to his hand anyway. Adam glanced from my eyes to my lips and back again. I held my breath. I knew what he was going to do—he waited for a signal, any signal. If I moved just an inch he would've been a happy boy. I was stricken. Adam was what I wanted. I'd taken one look at him at the hotline and knew he would be mine. I enjoyed the chase and now the chase was done. Adam was mine. So why wasn't I happy? Giddy? I was just…nothing.

Then I glanced over Adam's shoulder and knew it would have to wait. Kates was at our table.

"What the—?" I straightened away from Adam and stepped around.

"What?" He looked too and froze in place.

I wasn't sure why he seemed paralyzed, but I know that the sight of Kates whispering into Bennett's ear wasn't going to make my life any easier. What in the hell was she doing here? I didn't wait to ponder and marched across the room. "What are you doing here? And with *him*?"

Kates gasped, "What are you doing here?"

"I'm on a date." I jerked my thumb over my shoulder. Adam looked like he was caught in a pair of headlights.

"With him?"

Why was this so surprising?

"Yes. That's Adam. I told you he was mine." My chest puffed up a little bit.

"*That's* Adam?" Why was Kates so incredulous?

"Yes." I felt like a broken record.

A myriad of emotions flashed across her face. Shock, bafflement, disdain, and horror. I didn't care about the others, not really, but the horror caught me. I zeroed in and felt inside of her. What I felt made my toes curl.

Kates had a secret, a very shameful end-your-life type of secret. Bennett had told me that she was one of them, but I hadn't given him credit. I did now. The Lu— that she was loyal to wasn't Lucas. It was a vampire named Lucan. I remembered that two Families that had arrived in town, ready for a war. Lucan and Raitscliff. I highly doubted it was a coincidence. There were no coincidences when it came to the supernatural or to anything that regarded my life.

"Kates." It was all I could mutter. I was still dumbfounded by what was planned and I saw the veil fall over her eyes. She knew that I knew. She knew *how* I knew. That's when she grabbed my arm and held tight. Each of her fingers tightened over my elbow, but I couldn't look away.

"What are you going to do?" The question choked me.

"You weren't supposed to be here. You weren't supposed to be a part of this."

"But I am."

Her fingers tightened again. They would've hurt if they'd been from anyone except my best friend. "Don't."

She hung her head, but her fingers still held my arm immobile. Then she made a decision and barked at Bennett, "Take him."

Bennett nodded with an eager look in his eyes and rushed around me. He grabbed Adam and hauled him out of the restaurant.

"What's going on…?" Emily started to run after Bennett, but stopped and looked at us. She looked confused as she saw Kates. "Davy? What's going on… Kates?"

"Don't," I pleaded with Kates. I knew what was happening. I knew that Emily had seen too much, but I still tried.

Kates shook her head and strode forward. She clamped a hand on Emily and dragged both of us behind her. We burst into the cold air where a black van waited for us. The doors were open—beckoning and dark.

"Oh my god. No!" Emily cried out and dug her heels in.

She was no match for a vampire slayer. Kates tightened her hold and merely lifted Emily across the pavement and into the van. She let go of my arm in the process and I wasn't sure if it was accidental or not. It didn't matter. Kates started to climb into the van, but stopped and looked at me. I stood on the cold pavement, the chill bounced off my adrenaline, and I held my best friend's gaze steadfastly.

Emily cried behind her and Adam groaned in pain.

I could bolt and I knew Kates wouldn't chase after me. This was my best friend giving me a chance. I rubbed where she had held my elbow. It was a dull throb, but it didn't matter.

"Davy." Kates wanted me to run. She didn't want me to be a part of this—little did she know how much I *was* a part of it all.

I made my mind up in that second and strode forward. Kates dropped into a chair and I crossed over her to drop into the chair beside her. Emily and Adam shrank back in their seats. The door slammed shut and the van shot off down the street.

"We got him?" Bennett turned around from his front seat. I wasn't surprised to see a handgun in his hand, but did vampires even need weapons? I thought they were a weapon in themselves.

Kates reached to the floor and slammed a cartridge into her gun. "We got him, Benny."

"Alrighty tighty, man. That was fresh." Bennett grinned wolfishly, caught my look of disdain, and winked. "Come on, babe. You know our race. You've gotta appreciate how tight that was run."

"How tight that was run? Your race? Babe?" I questioned dully and leaned forward. "You really want to ask my opinion?"

Bennett cut an uneasy look towards Kates. "You hopped in all by yourself. No one made you come."

"Right, because when my friends are being kidnapped, I'd really appreciate the opportunity to run and hide. I'll remember that next time."

"You don't have to be such a bitch," Bennett muttered underneath his breath and turned back to look out the front window.

"What is going on? I don't understand—my arm really hurts," Emily moaned from the back.

Bennett smiled wolfishly.

"You like this, don't you." I was starting to *really* hate this vampire.

"Davy," Kates hushed me.

I shook off her restraining hand and narrowed my eyes. "You're like all the rest. You enjoy hurting people. You get off on it?"

Bennett chuckled and shook his head. "You mean like your ex-boyfriend? I knew him, you know."

"He wasn't my boyfriend," I snarled.

"That's what Craig used to say too." He didn't believe me at all.

"Bennett," Kates tried to hush him. It hadn't worked with me.

"You have horrible taste in men. Craig was fun to hang out with, but he was off his radar."

Emily squeaked. "What are you talking about, Bennett? What is he talking about, Davy? Kates?"

The only one not talking was Adam. I wondered why… and then I heard my answer from Kates as she turned to look at me. "We were sent to get the Immortal's boyfriend."

Adam seemed to shrink underneath her gaze. His hair was messed and his shirt was wrinkled. Then I saw the guilt in his eyes, in those adorable pure-kindness almond eyes. The anchor dropped. "What is she talking about?"

Bennett started to laugh.

"Shut up, Bennett!" Kates swiftly punched him.

Bennett seemed shocked and then he growled. It was an unearthly growl, a sound that only the undead could produce. The sound sent shivers down my back.

Emily shrieked.

I wanted Bennett dead, not silenced, but it didn't matter in that moment. I turned around, placed a hand on my seat, and felt the cold plastic material underneath my fingers. "Boyfriend?"

Adam flushed and hung his head in shame. "I… Shelly and I are dating."

Shelly and him—they were dating. The words met my ears, but I sat back, dazed, as I let them comprehend…. I liked Adam. I actually did, but… I didn't too… and I was so confused. Was this remorse that I was feeling?

"What'd I tell you? Bad taste in men. You should stick to my kind."

"Bennett, I swear that if you don't shut up, I will slice your head off!" Kates grated out.

"Your kind?" Emily moaned, tearful.

My throat burned, but when didn't it? I felt the first tingle in my stomach, deep inside, but I sucked in a ragged breath. Roane told me no Immortal stuff, certainly not with my current company. I wanted so badly to do something, to follow through with Kates' threat.

"You're one of us, Kates. Don't get all twisted and holy. You're in this all the way. Just like the rest of us. It's a tough break your buddy got brought along, but that's what you get for living in two worlds. You can't have it all, Katie."

"Do not call me Katie," Kates warned. Lethal.

Bennett laughed and turned back around.

I glanced at the driver. He'd remained quiet the entire time. I couldn't see his face at all, except a small side section. He was dressed in all black. A black baseball cap was pulled low over his eyes. It overshadowed the side of his face, but I caught a prominent cheekbone. Whoever he was, he had angular cheekbones. That was Kates' type. She liked her men lean and with those hollow cheeks.

"You said that you were sent for the Immortal's boyfriend. That's Adam?"

"Yeah." Kates frowned in sympathy. She raised a hand and I watched, immobile, as it descended in the air.

That's when I snapped. I gasped and caught her hand. "Don't you dare have pity on me. Don't you *dare* try to comfort me like a friend. You don't have that right. Don't you dare…."

Kates blanched.

I gripped harder.

I felt the pain slice through her arm. It flared in her sapphire eyes, but I didn't care. I sunk my fingers tighter in her arm until she cried out, "Davy, stop. Please…" She whimpered the last word.

Disgusted, I flung her arm away and sat back in my chair. I turned towards the window as I watched the scenery fly by.

In the back, Emily whimpered right alongside my betrayer. "Have we been kidnapped?"

"Yes, Emily," I murmured dully. "We've been kidnapped."

CHAPTER EIGHTEEN

We drove through town and stopped once to put blindfolds on. I thought Emily was going to hyperventilate, but Bennett skimmed a kiss over her forehead and she quieted. Even as the 'bad guy', he still had power over her. Then Kates turned and handed me the blindfold. I looked at it dumbly for a moment, but saw the appeal in her eyes. If I fought it, I wasn't sure if she would've overtaken me and put the blindfold on or if she would've allowed Bennett to do it. It didn't matter either way. I tied it behind my head and waited for Bennett to finish tying Adam's.

Adam. What could I even say about him? I couldn't think about him, not yet. I didn't even know what I thought anymore. Kates. Adam. Myself. Emily—betrayal was running rampant in these parts of Benshire.

After the blindfolds were checked a second time the van pulled ahead and we drove in silence the rest of the way. It slowed and turned upwards onto a gravel road. It wasn't long until we stopped and not one word was spoken.

The air felt heavy.

Suddenly, the door was thrown open and the cold blasted us. I flinched once, but refused to do it again.

"Come on, Davy," Kates urged softly.

I swallowed tightly and jumped out of the van. I felt Kates' alien touch as she grasped my arm and aligned herself to walk beside me. Emily whimpered behind me. Bennett shushed her in a seductive voice and then a door opened ahead of us and classical melodies greeted us. It seemed like an odd contrast, but the music echoed around us as we stood there. The place was large. Then I felt another ominous feeling start to tingle in my gut. Murmurs of conversation stopped when we stepped further into the room and I heard people, vampires?, stand up.

It was our entrance. Our hostage entrance—the thought struck me as amusing. I grinned, but I was instantly revolted at the idea that I might find something like this entertaining. Nothing was funny about the situation. Then I heard Emily's sobs of terror and sobered completely.

"Come on, Davy," Kates' restrained murmur hit my ears. Her request was unwelcome, but I couldn't fight back. I wanted to do something, to use my powers in someway… and then suddenly I was.

I gasped silently as I saw the room. My vision was slightly blurry with a dark reddish tint to it. I felt Kates look to her right and I saw that side of the room. That's when I realized that I still had my blindfold on. I wasn't seeing this through my eyes. I saw through Kates. I had slipped inside of her and was viewing the room through her eyes.

I had been right. The room *was* full of vampires. All of them stood and watched our slow trek. I instantly knew these vampires weren't from Benshire. They were dressed differently. Some wore leather vests. Some wore long flowing velvet red coats, fringed at the ends. Some dressed in feather tunics. Still others wore nothing except tight jeans. The one thing they had in common was a symbol that ran over the left arm and left shoulder. It was the letter L. That was the entire symbol, but it spoke volumes.

This was Lucan's Family.

I counted thirty on that side of the room before Kates glanced to the left and there I was. My head was bent. The blindfold was perfectly placed. I had a sneer of anger on my face. I smiled and watched as my lips tried to curve upwards, but failed. It didn't look pretty. I sighed and saw myself sigh. I wished Kates would look somewhere else.

She didn't and I felt remorse blast throughout Kates as we walked forward.

I tripped when my foot hit against a step and I saw nothing anymore. I stumbled out of her and concentrated on the stairwell. It curved upwards for two flights of stairs. We went down a hallway and then climbed another set of stairs. It felt more like a mausoleum. There was a dull swish across the floor ahead of us and I knew it was the sound of a heavy door being opened.

Kates led me inside and released my arm. A second later the door closed and I waited, holding my breath. When nothing else happened, I lifted my blindfold. I rapidly blinked as my eyes adjusted to our surroundings. The room was dark so I crossed to the wall and felt for a light switch. As my fingers ran across a cold plastic box, I felt the outline of a switch and flipped it up.

Light surrounded us.

We'd been put in a room that looked like a museum display. A huge king-sized bed stood in one corner with gold posts that led and hooked to a sheer canopy. It dipped halfway to the ground.

I counted six chairs that looked like thrones. Each of them was upholstered with red velour material. It reminded me of medieval times and I almost expected a court jester to dance out from behind one.

"What?" Emily gasped and whirled in a tight circle with her blindfold still on.

I rolled my eyes and reached to remove it. She shrieked until she saw that I held the blindfold in my hand.

"Oh." She sounded a little disappointed.

"You need to drop that guy, Em." It wasn't a suggestion.
She flushed and hung her head. "I know, but I'm weak and I think I'm on a little something."
Think? She was.

Adam groaned from the corner and I turned to see that he had sat on a chair. He gripped his blindfold tight in his hand and didn't look at us. No one said anything for a moment. It was almost as if there was too much to say that we didn't know where to start.

Then Emily exclaimed, "We've been kidnapped! I can't believe it. Why? Are they doing it for ransom? What's going on? Why are you so calm, Davy?"

I ignored Emily for the moment and stood in front of Adam. He saw the tips of my ballet slippers and gulped. His jaw clenched before he lifted his eyes to mine. There it was. I saw it in his eyes. I knew a cheater when I saw one.

"You're with Shelly?" I asked it quietly, but so damning.

Guilt was all over him, but he rasped out, "I didn't... I didn't mean for any of this to happen. Shelly was lonely and crying the other night when we went out with that guy. You kissed him and I... I got so jealous. I kissed Shelly. Your friend, Kates, saw us. She was going into the Shoilster and caught us."

I frowned. That explained... some of it.

They'd said the Immortal and the Immortal's boyfriend. Adam had looked guilty... none of this made sense. "Adam, they took us because of you. You know that, right? They grabbed you first."

"Because Kates is psychotic!" Emily laughed hysterically. She rounded to perch precariously on a dark purple velvet couch beside Adam's throne. She shook her head and her hand lifted to pull at the ends of her hair. "She was probably so angry that he was two-timing you that she seduced Bennett. She persuaded him to kidnap us all. It's all because of her."

My roommate was crazy, stupid, *and* under the influence of vampire lust.

Adam frowned, but didn't address Emily's weird ramblings. Instead, he sounded sincere. "I am so sorry, Davy. The thing with Shelly happened so quick and then I asked you out yesterday. I never thought you'd actually say yes. You were with that guy, even though you said that the kiss was just because of his girlfriend. And then you said you liked me and I liked you too—I *like* you. I still like you, but this happened... and... I was going to break up with Shelly tonight. I just didn't call her yet."

Well, if my math added correctly, I highly doubted he would've gotten in touch with her. Kates and the Lucan Family thought Adam was the Immortal's boyfriend. I knew that Roane had the Immortal. Everything should've added up so that meant—Shelly was the girl that Talia had brushed arms with the night before she jumped. They thought Shelly was the Immortal.

"But why kidnap you?" I asked the question out loud to myself, but I jumped when Emily answered.

"Kates is behind all of this. I already told you that. She's doing this to get even with Adam because she thinks he cheated on you. She's crazy. Your friend is crazy."

The crazy one was the one talking. I sighed and closed my eyes. My insides were a whirlwind. Everything was happening too fast and not fast enough. "None of this makes sense."

"What guy?" Emily must've finally heard Adam.

"Huh?" Adam looked at her.

"You said that Davy kissed a guy. Who? She only likes you." Could my roommate be more blunt?

"Emily," I hissed. "Shut up."

Adam frowned, ever so helpful. "I never got his name. We were never introduced, but he was tall."

"These people…," Emily murmured, tearful. "What kind of people could do this?"

Kidnappers. Heartless soulless people. Vampires.

I watched as my roommate tried to make sense of what she couldn't understand. She really thought Bennett was a person, someone with a soul. She didn't understand the power he had over her. She clung to what she wanted to believe. And Adam—he just saw his own guilt. I felt a tear at the corner of my eye, but I swallowed painfully and brushed it away. Adam was the guy that I had thought all along. He was so human that he was… human. He got jealous. He made a mistake. Then he got caught up in the situation. Neither of them had a clue what was really going on. I was envious of their naiveté. It was my fault Emily was crying. It was my fault that Adam looked so shameful. Both of them were innocent in this entire thing.

I was the Immortal.

Then the door was pushed open. Emily jumped, but she didn't squeal this time. Thankfully.

Adam looked up.

"Davy," Kates called me. A strand of her dirty blonde hair had slipped down to frame the corner of her cheek. Her sea blue eyes were bright and clear. She fully knew what she was doing. There was no vampire lust that filtered her decisions.

I took a small breath. I needed to accept the inevitable. Kates had betrayed me, but the sad part was that she didn't know she betrayed me. I did know one thing, though. Kates wasn't there to kill vampires. She was there for an entirely different reason.

"Come on," she beckoned and I went.

CHAPTER NINETEEN

We didn't go far. We went down one set of steps and past four doors before Kates opened the fifth. After she shut the door and I glanced around, I realized that this was her room. There was a giant bed that had a canopy, just like the one in the other room. There was a sensual feeling to the room until I caught sight of the opened closet door. I saw the hooker boots, leather halter tops, and frayed jeans.

That was all Kates.

"This is where you stay?" I asked, hurt.

Sorrow flashed in her eyes, but she nodded before she perched on another velour throne chair. She only had two. It looked like they kept the good stuff for the hostages.

"So… let's start this by you telling me why you *really* came to Benshire." I deadlocked my eyes with hers. This was the showdown. Truth time.

Kates swallowed once. "I came here because I fell in love with someone."

"Someone or something?" I couldn't keep the disdain away.

Anger flashed briefly in her eyes, but she pushed past it. "I fell in love with a vampire. Your contempt's not new so could you stop with the attitude? It's not helping."

"It's helping me."

"You want some answers and I'm trying to tell you them. I won't be so inclined if you piss me off."

"Listen to you. 'So inclined'—who've you been talking to? You don't talk like that on a good day, Kates. Drop the act. I want my friend here, not whoever you are when you're with this *thing* you love."

"Thing?"

Had we just not gone over this? Contempt. Me. For vampires. Not a surprise. I raised my chin and glared.

"What is your problem? You're acting like I've lied to you!" Kates shouted.

"You have!" I shouted right back. "You just kidnapped me."

"You weren't supposed to be there!"

"Well, I was. And my roommate is in that room. And Adam—it had to be Adam?"

Kates snorted again, but laughed hollowly. "Don't come crying to me because you have crap taste in guys."

My eyes went red. "Excuse me?"

"You didn't like Craig, but he sure liked you. Maybe it's something about you that attracts these losers?"

"Losers? Me? Are we really not considering your vampire? He's a creature of the night, Kates. I don't think Adam is worse than that."

"Creature of the night? So am I, Davy!"

"You're a human." Unlike myself.

"So are you."

"This isn't about me."

"This *is* about you! I'm sorry that you're mad that Adam cheated on you. You could do better. He looks like a pussy."

She'd been the one to interrupt Adam and Shelly while I'd been pressing Roane against the wall around the corner… was it hot in here or was it me? I fingered my shirt's collar and pulled it away to fan myself, but to no avail—I was burning up. I hoped my Immortal stuff wasn't acting up.

"You're going to be fine anyway."

"What do you mean?"

"Look," Kates continued. "I came to Benshire because of the Immortal."

"The fairytale Santa Claus for vampires?" Her words exactly.

Kates grimaced and I caught a flash of embarrassment. "That girl that killed herself, she was the Immortal."

Tell me about it.

"I was sent here to find the new Immortal."

At her look of expectation, my eyes widened and I sat up straight. I was supposed to be confused. I was supposed to be shocked. I was supposed to be... I didn't care. "Like I'm going to believe anything you say right now anyway."

"Oh my god, Davy!"

"You kidnapped me!"

"I did not!" Kates surged to her feet.

"Evidence. I'm in a vampire castle! Against my will!"

"By chance! By chance. It was an accident. You're not supposed to be here. You're not supposed to be a part of this at all."

I wasn't supposed to be a part of this? She had no idea. "I'm still here, aren't I?"

"Could you be more dramatic? I'm here. I'm going to protect you. Obviously."

"Right," I scoffed and crossed my arms. "Because you're a slayer?"

"Because I'm your best friend," Kates pointed out. "Idiot."

"How'd you even know where we were?"

She grimaced. "Bennett knew. He followed Adam to your dorm and overheard him talking to Emily."

Oh holy hell.

She added, "For what it's worth, I think Bennett actually has a thing for her."

"What else should I know about, Kates? You were supposed to be at Blue's this whole time. Did you even go? What happened with that?"

Her eyes widened and I held my breath. This was not good.

"I went," Kates murmured quietly, reluctantly. "But you told me that she'd gone inside and did her empathic thing. I couldn't have that, Davy."

"*I* did it," I wrung out, hoarse.

"You're my best friend. That's different… and I know you, Davy. You don't really—you're not really detail-oriented, you know. You only go so far. I haven't been worried about you, but Blue—she—she knew things that she shouldn't have."

"What did you do to her?" My hands started to tremble. I felt my voice quiver and I felt something become unglued inside of me… it was starting to rise, starting to choke…. I stopped breathing. "Is she alive?"

"Barely." She whispered the word and refused to meet my eyes.

Blue was family. "What did you do?"

Roane said not to get upset—too late for that. I was upset. I was more than upset. Kates said nothing and I jerked forward a step. "What did you do, Kates?!"

I felt her guilt before I heard it. I closed my eyes and whirled away as I saw what she'd done. She'd hit her. I flinched as I heard the punch. I felt the fist crunch against Blue's jaw. My sponsor hadn't stood a chance. "She respected your privacy. She wouldn't tell me what she'd felt. She was worried about you and she wanted you to get help. She wanted to be the person to help you. I trusted you to go to her! What did you do, Kates?!"

"You know!" Kates screamed back.

I felt the slap of her words. I doubled over and gasped for breath. Tears came to my eyes and I rapidly blinked them away. "You don't know what you've done."

Kates looked like she'd just been slapped by my words.

"Where is she?"

"She's in the hospital. Coma."

"You're a first class bitch."

'I am.'

I heard Kates' thought.

'I deserve so much worse. I should be the one in the coma. I should be—no, Lucan needs me. He said that I'd have to do things I wouldn't want to.

He always knows. He said this would happen and Davy would react like this. He knows.'

"Who the hell is Lucan?"

Kates jerked her head up and her eyes widened. "You can—no, you can't!"

I stalked forward, one step at a time.

She backed away. "You can't, there's no way. You never could before…"

"I'm gifted, remember?"

"This isn't… you're not *that* gifted, Davy."

I pierced her eyes. I wanted her to feel me deep inside, so deep that she'd never feel privacy again. "Maybe I've never been this furious before. Maybe I never had a reason to do what I can do now. She was like a mother, Kates. She was like my mother!"

She wanted to deny what I said. She wanted to not believe me, but it didn't matter. "Are you going to tell me who Lucan is? Or am I going to go inside of you and figure it out myself?"

She blanched at my meaning. A cruel smile curved at the corners of my mouth. I wanted to see her squirm some more.

"I'm Lucan." I heard the answer, but it came from the doorway.

I swung my gaze and stopped short. He was Roane's complete double. He had the same coal eyes that held too many promises. Some of those promises sent shivers down my back. It was the same angular cheekbones, strong jaw line, and full plump lips that begged to be touched. He even had the same cocky, yet saddened, shrug to his muscular shoulders. They were strong shoulders. Both of them stood the same. Confident. Leaders. Sure that their way was the right way.

Except, there were differences too. Roane kept his hair buzzed short. Lucan wore his black hair sleek and straight to where it touched the tips of his shoulders. I watched as he lifted a graceful hand and tucked it behind one ear and knew that was his habit.

Kates watched in yearning and her hand jerked. She wanted to be the one to tuck that strand of hair behind his ear.

"She loves you."

Kates jerked her gaze to me and instantly looked away, but I already saw it. I saw everything.

I breathed out, "You weren't thinking of Roane before. You were thinking of him. Blue got it wrong somehow. Then in the car, you and Roane, you two looked like you wanted to murder each other. It was because of…" I swung my gaze to Lucan. "Who are you?"

He smiled, almost tenderly, but I still saw the killer in him. "Lucas is my twin brother—my *human* twin brother."

'Raitscliff and Lucan have both found a girl… their families are here'

Lucan strolled forward. "We're both vampires, yes. We were sired from different families."

"What do you want from me?" I wasn't sure how to react. In fact, I wasn't sure how to even breathe around this Roane look-alike. Lucan smiled again and I saw another difference. They lived by different codes. Roane defied death. He stood in the way of death and Lucan, he merely thought death couldn't touch him. I wasn't sure which one was the safest for company, but I'd soon find out.

"You're Kates' best friend. You got mixed up in this by accident. She says that you know Lucas, so I have a mission for you." He really didn't think I'd decline the proposal, little did he know about who I was.

I tilted my chin up. "What do you want?"

He turned and held Kates' gaze for a moment, but neither of them needed to communicate their thoughts. I read the look and knew it was a lovers' connection.

"Lucas has the Immortal at his home. I want you to go there and give her a message. I want you to tell her that we have her boyfriend. If she doesn't want him to die, she needs to come to us by tomorrow night."

"And if she doesn't?"

"We'll have a meal. That's all."

Kates jerked in reaction.

I stepped forward. "And what makes you think that 'Lucas' will let me talk to her?"

Then he smiled one of those intimate I-know-your-secret smiles. "Because I know that this Adam character isn't your boyfriend."

"How do you know that?" I already knew. I *so* already knew. Though, I needed to hear it.

"Because I smell my twin brother all over you. You'll have no problem getting in to see the Immortal and we both know it."

Well… hell.

CHAPTER TWENTY

"You know what to do, right?" Kates asked as she walked me to the van.

"Lie to the Hunter and tell Shelly that her boyfriend's going to die if she doesn't give her blood up to the longest fang."

Kates sighed, annoyed. "Come on, Davy. This is some serious stuff here."

Oh, believe me. I knew the gravity of my situation. "I wouldn't want anyone to end up in a coma. Yeah, I get how serious this is."

"I know that you're upset about what happened with Blue, but… things just happened. I didn't mean for that to happen, but it did and I'm going to do everything I can to make sure your friends are okay."

Oh gee, thanks for the consideration. "You're right. I *am* more than upset about what you did to Blue. You didn't mean for it to happen? What'd you mean for, Kates? You have a temper. You don't think I know that? I should probably be grateful that you didn't just kill Blue. That would've solved your problem, right? She peaked inside you and saw the real you, so you kill her."

"Shut up!" Kates snarled. "Just… shut up. You don't know—" *'Lucan knows. He knows me. He told me to kill Blue and I couldn't, but it's okay. It worked out. He said that no one could make the connection, not until after… he said everything would be alright. I have to trust him. I love him.'*

I watched as Kates calmed herself down. Lies. "Wow, Kates. You take the cake. Is this about you loving this guy or is this about you not being alone?"

She'd been the one to introduce Craig and me. She'd told me to set Craig on fire. She'd been the one who told me that fire wouldn't kill him, but it'd hurt him. I had wanted to hurt him. I wanted to hurt him still. A stab of nausea surged through me. All my regrets, shadows, the darkest time in my life—and Kates had been right beside me the entire time. She'd been the one to encourage me, but now that I thought about it, she might not have encouraged me in the right way.

I expected blistering rage from Kates. I got patience instead and I blinked, startled, as she relayed almost warmly, "I love him. He's… he's going to change things, make things how they're supposed to be. I know you can't understand because you don't know anything about this world and you shouldn't. It's a dark world, but Lucan's going to change things, make things right."

"So that you can kill vampires again?" I scoffed at the idea. The decree was finalized and it swept over the entire vampire nation. There was no reversing that baby.

"Maybe."

I saw her belief and couldn't believe it. She thought that, she *really* thought that. I didn't know some stuff about the vampire world, but I knew enough to know that the decree was set in stone. There'd be a few world wars within the vampire community before that decree was overthrown… unless….

'It just means that vampire has too much power. No creature should have that power.'

I sucked in a choking breath. I suddenly, very suddenly, needed to get to Roane. This was the 'world at stake' feeling that I felt the night on the roof with Talia. Something had happened, something very, very wrong had happened and I felt it. I had ignored it. Now things might've gone too far to stop it.

"I have to go," I rushed out and darted to the van. The door was open so I hopped inside and slammed it behind me. I never stopped to look at who drove me. I just needed to get to Roane, but I'd need to go to the dorm first.

Once I hurled myself through the lobby, up the stairs, and down the hall, I burst through the door. I was grateful that I'd been the last out the door and not Emily because I never locked the door. Emily had been too frazzled by her date, she'd forgotten her purse—that meant her phone.

I scrolled through until I found Roane's number. It took a few rings, but he answered, "Is this Emily?"

"No, it's me. I lost my phone, but that's not why I'm calling. I have to see you, now!" Please, please don't ask for any explanation. I didn't have time.

Roane hesitated a second and then asked, "Where are you?"

"My dorm room."

"I'll send Gregory."

"Thank you, thank you, thank you." I needed to calm down, but I was bursting at the seams. As I waited, I couldn't sit still. I paced. I jogged in place. I did jumping jacks. I even rearranged the furniture. Afterwards, I cringed. Emily wouldn't want the couch by the window.

"Davy? It's Gregory. Lucas said to knock on your door…"

"Coming!"

Gregory greeted me with a polite nod and I tried to ignore the attention this *very* large Viking vampire was attracting. His voice could've rumbled through the entire building. Heads popped out from nearly every door, but while some squeaked in fear, a lot squeaked from excitement—the sexual kind.

Vampire. Horny freshman girls. What else needed to be said?

Gregory swept around me in the lobby and held each of the doors open until we got to the car. It was the same black SUV that he'd driven before. "Can't you drive a car with some color? Why does it always have to be black?"

"Davy?"

"Nothing. Nevermind." I shrugged it off and slipped inside. From there, it was all foot tapping, knuckle breaking, and counting my breaths again.

I felt like I needed to burst, like something inside of me finally knew something—or felt something was going to happen. I was going to burst from the inside out. I just knew it. Then Gregory pulled the car over and I burst out of the car to sprint inside. I swept past Wren and a whole host of other vampires.

They were all arriving for the war.

I darted up the stairs and spotted Roane's closed bedroom doors. I threw them open, prepared to unburden my soul, but I braked abruptly. Nothing. Roane wasn't there. The sheets were in the same place. The window was open and a cool breeze swept in.

"Oh my god! Vampires are so unreliable!" I cried to myself.

Then I heard a soft chuckle behind me and I whirled around—my jaw dropped. There he was, buttoning a black shirt that looked custom-fitted and straight from the dry cleaners. He wore a pair of light blue jeans underneath, which also looked custom fitted and dry-cleaned.

"You've got money. I can see that," I stated as my greeting.

"That's what you had to say and why you called with your commanding 'now!'?" Roane drawled as he slipped past only to drop the shirt off his shoulders—oh whoa. I had assumed he'd been buttoning it up, but nope. He'd been unbuttoning it.

"Wha—why—what are you doing?" I quickly turned around. I wanted to look. I shouldn't. It was bad to look, but I peeked anyway. Roane was all muscles. Perfect, chiseled, hard ridges, muscles up and down and all around. My fingers itched to touch them and my mouth went dry, but I twitched to keep myself back.

"I was out. I had to make sure you and Gregory weren't followed."

"That would've been bad, huh? If they had followed me…" I trailed off as Roane was in front of me in a flash… in all his shirtless glistening chest gloriousness…. Fans. Vampires should keep fans everywhere they were… for all those hot, passionate, and overheated humans like myself….

"They?" Roane caught my shoulders and jerked me back to him. I'd been absentmindedly looking for a fan somewhere.

"They?" he barked again.

"They." I needed to remind myself who 'they' were. Oh—"Yes. Your twin brother." I growled that last bit and shoved Roane back. "You could've told me that you had a twin brother. They have Emily and Adam."

"You met Lucan?" Roane grilled. "You talked to Lucan?"

I nodded. "I met him. I talked to him. I found out that Kates is in love with him, thanks for that heads up and yes—he sent a message for the Immortal. I'm supposed to deliver it because *apparently* he can smell you all over me. That's gross. I really don't like being sniffed."

"I've almost forgotten what he smells like," Roane confessed as he moved around me and back into the bedroom. He flicked his wrist out and shut the door on his way. As I turned to watch him, the door shut behind me with a click.

"That's… how can you forget what your twin smells like? Wouldn't he smell like you?" I couldn't believe I was having this conversation.

Roane stopped, stared at me for a moment, and then crossed to his closet. He pulled out a grey shirt, but only held it as he hung his head. "Lucan and I were sired by different Families. That means that we have the same face now. Nothing else remains the same with the two of us. I have different blood than he does."

"Because you were sired by different Families?"

"Lucan was sired first." Roane still hadn't put the shirt on. He only held it and now his hand wrapped tightly around it. He looked at the floor and I heard the suffering in his voice. "He was the louder one of us. Everyone thought he was the leader. When he was sired… I felt it happen. I felt him and then suddenly—I thought he was dead. It was almost two weeks before he came to me. He said that he couldn't control himself before that and he wanted to make sure he wouldn't hurt me. I didn't see much of Lucan after he became a vampire. I lived another year as a human until this man came to me."

I felt the history swirl around us, like it was another entity in the room.

Roane continued, haunted, "He told me that Lucan had become a problem with the vampires. He was uncontrollable and defying a lot of their rules. He said that I was once his twin brother. They wondered if I could help them with their problem. That's what they called him. My brother was 'their problem.'"

I heard his hollow laugh and bit my lip from crying out.

"He turned you into a vampire because of your brother?"

"No. He took me to Lucan—as a human. Lucan was the one who decided I should be a vampire. He missed me. He wanted me beside him. He wanted things to be how they were. The man who had come to me realized what Lucan was about to do. He did it instead. To say Lucan was furious is an understatement. He ripped my Master's head off."

"So…" I asked, hesitant, "You didn't have a Master?" I had no idea what that meant, but I guessed that it meant something.

He cleared his throat. "I joined Lucan for awhile. I became a part of his Family, even though I wasn't from their bloodline. The rest of the group didn't like that, but Lucan was their leader. They did what he said and I'd been his twin brother—it still meant something to Lucan and me. We were how we used to be, for a time."

Inseparable. I heard it before he said it. I felt it from him. Roane wished things were how they used to be.

"As I learned things, I started to change. Lucan didn't like it at first, but I don't know—I think his Family were the ones who stepped in."

"You said Lucan was the 'louder' one of you. They thought he was the leader."

Roane shook his head and sat. His shirt was still fisted in his hands before him. "I'd been the leader when we were human. Lucan was just loud, but he didn't think things through. He acted for me sometimes. I liked controlling from behind the scenes and it worked for us. We were starting to get back to that and I think his Family didn't like the idea that one of their own wasn't the leader anymore. They didn't like being led by an outsider. Lucan loved it. I took them to new heights. I told you that I'd done the torture with their Family I'd done worse than that. I didn't know who I was. I felt a separation between me and Lucan. I hated it. I went dark, really dark… as a vampire."

"Until they kicked you out."

"Lucan was forced to kick me out…," Roane closed his eyes. "I found my Family and things changed… for awhile."

"Was that the last time you saw him, when he kicked you out?"

He shook his head, his jaw clenched. "I wish, but… no. Lucan and I… we still both liked to defy laws, even vampire laws. That was in us from when we were human. We still saw each other until…"

"Lucas," I whispered, but held back. I wasn't sure… He was going to say something, but hesitated. And something in me didn't want to hear it.

He swung his eyes to mine and I couldn't look away. It was… he was starving. I was starving… something was in the air—I couldn't move. I couldn't breathe. I couldn't… I couldn't think.

"You called me by my name," he wrung out. Hoarse.

I nodded with a tight throat. I couldn't form any words. I couldn't talk… I had gravitated to him and I stood above him as he sat. I… I didn't know what to say, how to react. I needed to be by him… it was something in me or maybe it was just me. I could only breathe. That was all I focused on until I felt his hand lift and the back of his finger wiped a tear away from me.

"Davina," he whispered as he arched upwards, but he didn't seek my lips. Not yet.

I grasped the side of his face and I was the one to press my lips to his. A part of me knew that I needed him and I wouldn't ever stop needing him. I just hoped it wasn't the end of both of us.

CHAPTER TWENTY-ONE

I pressed against him, as close as possible. His hand slid slowly up my back and lingered at my shoulder. He traced his finger down my arm, to my wrist, my hand, my fingertip, until it rested warmly on my stomach. He spread his palm wide and held me in place for a second.

I gasped and surged upward against him. I needed air.

Roane groaned as he pulled his lips away. "Your shield's down."

I pressed my lips against his and moaned when I felt the struggle inside of him. He paused. He wanted to say something, but my tongue gently touched the tip of his. Then he lost the battle for control. Both his hands claimed my head and he tilted it so his tongue swept further, deeper.

I was so lost in his exploration that I hadn't realized when Roane lifted me in the air. As I felt the satin sheets underneath my bare skin my eyes shot open.

When had I gotten undressed?

Roane's lips settled on my neck and I felt the throb pound furiously inside of me—it didn't matter when I'd gotten undressed.

He rested just above me and cradled the back of my neck. He lingered just over my collarbone, but swept his lips gently back and forth before he settled down to suckle lightly. I swept a hand up into his hair and the other explored down his chest to rest on his belt buckle. My fingers paused and then dipped inside. Roane growled as he surged upwards.

I laid there on the bed as he stood between my legs and both of us froze in place.

Then I felt something come over us. I didn't know what it was, but I knew I didn't want it there. My hand fell away from his jeans with lightning speed. He caught it and held it. My eyes locked with his and I found myself thinking, *'What?'*

'Your shield shouldn't be down.' How could a thought be so accusing?

'We're in the middle of something and you want to lecture me on my shield? Really? Is this the time?'

'Your shield should always be raised. You don't know who could get in.'

'Besides evil vampires who want to drain my blood? I have no idea.'

"Enough," Roane snarled viciously. I jumped from the sound. "Raise your shield now! I shouldn't be able to read your thoughts."

"What's the deal?" I sat up, but Roane didn't move. The movement brought us closer, only a few inches separated us. I swallowed tightly. My body reacted so quickly.

"The deal is that someone else, someone who doesn't want to protect you could get inside and read your thoughts," Roane leaned over and whispered, intimately.

A shiver sent goose bumps over my skin. *'Why would I worry about some evil vampire getting in my head when you're already there?'*

Roane didn't react—outwardly. He didn't show a thing, but I felt him. He was all fury. It blasted against me. Acid dripped from his voice. "Right."

"I…" I scrambled up, but stopped abruptly.

Roane jerked his head back and to the side.

I jumped in reaction from his quickness. When he didn't move back, I waited—something needed to be said or done or exploded. I wasn't sure what I voted for, but… just something.

"You're angry."

I hadn't expected that. I blinked in shock at the understanding in his voice. "Uh…"

Roane turned his head back and his dark eyes caught mine. "You don't understand this. You, me, and you're angry."

"Are you serious?" I snarled back at him, but I felt a traitorous tremor build in my body. It wanted release. It demanded release, but… nothing.

"This… attraction we have for each other—it's like a pull."

How quaint. "Is that what it is? I hadn't noticed."

Roane moved back a step. I felt his hands leave my thighs where they'd been resting. The cold invaded…. "You were hunted by a vampire, my kind. I feel it too, Davy. We can barely be in the same room without touching. It's been there since the beginning and it's been growing every minute. It's almost uncontrollable lately, but— this is new to you."

And it wasn't to him?!

I sat up straighter and stood slowly. "So are you the big bad experienced vampire lover and I'm the virgin? Are you here to teach me what I need to know? Or maybe your job is to guide me correctly, make sure I don't fumble along. Right? Am I getting this wrong?"

"You're hearing me wrong," he said faintly. Defeated.

I stood tall, shrugged my shoulders back, and firmed my jaw. "I hope so because you're sounding pretty damn superior."

"That's not what I'd intended…"

"That's not what you intended? This whole thing wasn't intended. I shouldn't have gone up to that roof. I shouldn't have answered that phone. I shouldn't have a best friend who's a brainwashed bunny by your 'human' twin and I really shouldn't be here with you. None of this should've happened. I shouldn't have even come to Benshire, but I listened to Blue."

I stopped and gasped for air, my eyes wild. Then I choked out, "She should've picked someone else. I can't be this Immortal. I don't want to have this on my shoulders. I can't—someone else should be the Immortal. I haven't had this for a few days and already my roommate was kidnapped. My best friend is in love with a vampire that wants to drain me and… my empath sponsor is in a coma. I don't even know what to say about you."

Something happened and I felt like I could breathe again.

Roane moved closer, but he paused. "I hurt your pride before. I'm sorry. All I meant is that you know *of* my world, but you don't *know* my world. Now you're the Immortal and your entire life needs to change. You're right. Being the Immortal is a lot to bear. It's a great burden, but you're also wrong. Talia didn't choose you. The Immortal thread chose you. Talia trusted the Immortal thread to choose the right person—it did. It chose you for a reason, Davy."

"I really don't want to be the Immortal, Lucas. I want—can't I pass it along?" I was still a little miffed.

He didn't answer for a moment. "You can't. Once the Immortal thread is linked with your body, you'll die when it passes to the next carrier. The body goes through a withdrawal that's lethal. Talia didn't want—she didn't want to suffer like that."

I closed my eyes swiftly and felt everything from that night again. She'd chosen her death... now I understood, but I still wished I hadn't. I wrung out, "I just want to wake up and hear Emily snoring. I don't want this. I can't have this."

I slowly dropped back down on the bed and cradled my head in my hands. My fingers slid through my hair and clung to each strand. I wanted to pull them out. I wanted to feel something other than what I was feeling. I couldn't deal with it.

Roane reached forward and delicately moved my knee aside. He knelt before me.

I held my breath.

He moved his hand from my leg and slowly reached to untangle my hands from my hair. I gasped as the last finger was detangled and then my fingers desperately sought his shoulders. He slid in and I surged forward to wrap my arms tighter around him.

"You have to bear something that you didn't choose. I understand, Davy. I understand it more than you think." Roane tucked his head against mine. His lips brushed the tip of my ear. "I know what it's like to have your life suddenly change and it's not what you decided. I do understand that."

I frowned.

His hand curved around my neck and I felt the cool touch of his lips when he pressed a kiss to my ear. "You can do this, Davy. We'll figure everything else out."

Did I dare believe him? I wanted to—badly. I lifted my head, met his black eyes, and smoothed my thumb over his cheek. "I'm a little moody right now. I'm not used to being… so powerless. I hate it."

He didn't say anything. Then he dipped and touched his lips to mine.

I closed my eyes and felt it again. It had been rushed and fevered, but the wave of lust swirled slowly throughout me. The heat spread from my fingertips, up my arms, down my sides, around my toes, and back to settle in my center.

I entwined my arms around his neck.

Roane grazed his lips against mine, hypnotically back and forth. I arched upward, needing more. As my neck was stretched to the fullest, he slid his mouth down my neck and settled on my collarbone where he started to suckle.

My hand cradled the back of his neck and my other slid over his shoulders, feeling the hard dip between his muscles until it rested on his hip. Roane continued to suckle and I pressed down on his head, just lightly.

It inflamed him. He swiftly lifted me up to place me on the bed.

I laid there; dazed at how quick he'd reacted, but Roane didn't wait for my brain to catch up. He shucked his pants and quickly unzipped mine. As they slid down my legs and past my toes, I panted for breath. After he dropped them on the ground, Roane crouched over me. His eyes met mine, captive and fevered.

Then with a tug at his lips, he slid a hand up my leg. Sharp desire pierced me, but I could only gasp for breath and lay there, nearly paralyzed. I watched, entranced, as his hand slid to my waist, caressed my stomach for a moment, and then dipped between my legs. As a finger entered me, my paralysis was gone. I shot up from the bed and wrapped my arms around his shoulders. I threw one leg around his hip. Roane grasped it and raised it higher. His finger slipped further inside and I could only cling as it started to move in and out.

The sensations built quickly. He kept moving, in and out, until I gasped and turned my mouth towards his shoulder. My lips grazed his skin and in a drunken state I pressed my teeth against his skin.

Roane groaned roughly.

I nipped his skin—he shuddered. I licked him and he slid two fingers inside of me.

My fingers dug into him, starving. Then I bit—quickly and savagely. I needed more, but I didn't know of what.

Roane arched his head and growled. I felt the reverberations between my legs and then I moaned as Roane quickly positioned himself and entered smoothly. At his first thrust, I wrapped my legs around his waist and hooked my ankles.

The pleasure intensified and I couldn't think. I couldn't do anything except hold on as the fever built and built.

Roane bent his head down and found my collarbone again where he started to suckle. His teeth grazed against my skin and he nipped lightly when he thrust deep at the same time. The pace quickened, in and out, back and forth.

I groaned, but bit my lip to silence my moans.

"No," Roane gasped and lifted himself off of me so his weight didn't press down anymore.

I protested and tried to draw him back down.

He held me off and I bit down harder on my lips as he pistoned into me. Deftly, Roane slid his thumb between my lips and bent down to whisper, "Bite down on me, not on yourself."

I didn't register the desperation in his voice, but I felt the pleading through my body. And, answering something carnal, my teeth pierced his skin.

Roane cradled my head and quickened his pace. We were both lost, only feeling each other.

I felt his blood slide down my throat and gasped, needing more.

Roane held me tighter against him, almost crushing me, but I welcomed it. I needed it. I was starved for more—and then the fever built. I was on the edge—Roane grasped my hip, pulled out, and slammed back inside. Both of us went hurdling over the edge. The waves took over my body. I collapsed on the bed and was powerless as the ripples coursed through me. Then slowly my eyelids fluttered shut.

CHAPTER TWENTY-TWO

"It's the three ring circus. There are clowns, tigers, one legged elephants, and for a bonus feature: we've got a white zebra. You in for the count? You want tickets with that heaping bowl of popcorn? Deal's going once, twice, too late."

Only one voice said things like that—I sighed and sat up in the darkness. "I'm sleeping… again."

"Again—you mean 'finally'!" It chided me, "You've been awake for a very long time. It's about time you fell off to nanaland. I can only amuse myself so much here. You're not that entertaining of a person."

"Thanks… for that."

"Keeping it real, Bearded Lady."

Oh, lovely. A circus theme.

"Fairytales are overdone. The court jester wants his turn."

"Last time you told me I'm the Immortal. I've adjusted. I'll do whatever I need. What else can you hit me with? I'd like to wake up or go back to normal dreams. You're a little hard to handle sometimes." If I tried to reason with it, would it work?

The voice laughed. Shrill. "Would you like a comb for your beard?"

No reasoning would be had. "So what are you here to enlighten me with?"

"You lie really well." The voice had been maniacal before, but it was calm, eerily calm now.

I felt shivers go down my back. "What are you talking about?"

"Ask your lover."

Roane's words lashed back at me before I could stop them. *Lying. All you do is lie.*

I flinched and murmured, "No. You're wrong."

"I haven't said anything," the voice gloated.

"I know what you're going to say. You're going to say what he said. I don't lie. I'm not a liar."

"Tigers spawn earthlings on their back. Sometimes they ride on the backs of elephants, but only the ones with roller skates."

"Make sense, for once!" I shrieked into the darkness. It was an abyss.

"Silly Bearded Lady. They don't ride on the one legged elephant. That'd be dangerous."

"I'm not lying to anyone."

"And stupid. Who'd want to ride on the back of a one legged elephant? You'd fall right off." The voice ignored me and continued, amused, "And then rolling hula hoops that are on fire would burn you. Why are they always on fire? I've never figured that out."

"Enough!" I'd forced it before and I was willing to bet that I could do it again.

A black wind shrieked in protest and swept around me. I blinked, startled, and tried to stand still as a tornado picked up from underneath my feet. It rushed upwards, enveloped me, and as it started to settle—I found myself staring back at… what a shocker—myself. Except that it wasn't me. My brown curls looked sleek and framed my shoulders. My eyes weren't innocent. They were knowing, wise, and a little crazy. And still, I looked sultry. I was dressed how I had dressed for Adam's date, in my lace shirt and snug jeans, but there was a different aura that surrounded the Immortal me. Confidence.

She grinned and winked. "Bet this isn't what you wanted, huh?"

"How'd you know?" I returned, sardonically. "It's not as if you're a part of me or something."

"You're sarcastic."

"Just because you're inside of me doesn't mean that you understand me."

The Immortal me smiled sweetly. "I know a lot more about you than you know about yourself. I know all about Craig. I know about Kates. I know how you're heaping a whole pile of denial poop on a burning house because you did the deed with a vampire. And not any vampire, Bearded Lady. You did it with *thee* vampire. There are ramifications that you can't handle right now."

It wouldn't stop. "Please, please. All this nonsense—I can't handle it. I might go insane."

"Every circus must pitch a tent and entertain."

"Let me guess, I'm your audience?"

"You're the tent, Beardy, but you'll do. The tigers might not think so. They might want to shave off your beard or burn the tent. I haven't decided which."

"I'd really like to wake up. I need to tell Roane something and I can't when I'm asleep."

"That's right, Horny Bearded Lady. You didn't stop to think. The tigers think it's funny how the Bearded Lady forgets her beard when she's around The World's Strongest Man."

"Oh, please. Roane is not the world's strongest man." I felt foolish saying that. Who said things like that?

"You might be surprised." The Immortal laughed it off and vanished.

Great—back to the dark abyss. There were no winds this time. It was just darkness, no mocking voice, and no uneasy feeling inside of my stomach.

I looked down and choked out a gasp. I lifted my arm and like before, I saw the same silver color underneath my skin. I watched in fascination as the silver color seemed to melt into a thick rich paste that sparkled like diamonds. I liked diamonds, just not inside of me.

"You're every girl's best friend. You're the prize, Davy. You're the one that everyone wants."

"Tell me something that I don't know," I challenged.

"Craig wanted to make you a vampire. He told you how he'd do it, how much he'd enjoy it, and that you'd thank him in the end.

And now—vampires, vampires all around the shiny prize. What's a scared little girl to do? The hungry monsters keep circling, but they won't be kept at bay for long. A shark's going to bite soon—or maybe one did."

"Roane didn't bite me. I bit him."

"You liked it. You'd do it again. I can feel the thirst inside of you. What's that mean? Are you going to become a vampire?" The Immortal laughed hysterically and spun around me in tight circles.

I looked down at my arms and watched, detached, as the sparkling paste thinned and became like blood. "Roane said you chose me, did you? Did you actually choose me or did you get stuck with me?"

"The divorce will have collateral damage that no fortune teller can foresee."

That was a cheerful thought. "What do you want from me?"

I felt the Immortal slow to a stop, instantly, and sensed its calm. "Stop lying to yourself. You're only hurting yourself."

"Fine," I gritted out. "You invaded me! You had no right."

"He's thee vampire. You should sit up and pay attention."

"How can I? Your riddles are a bit mind twisting," I snorted out.

Then it answered another one. "As long as you're the Immortal, you are unable to become a vampire."

I clasped my eyes closed in relief. Maybe there were some benefits to being the Immortal.

"You drank his blood. There are ramifications for that—ones that won't be foreseen until much later, but they'll still be there when you've forgotten your worry." Relief, release, and now doom.

"I'm tired. I want to wake up."

"Every circus has a snake charmer. Who's yours? What snake slithered in your tent?"

I gasped awake and bolted upright in bed. I didn't need to find my bearings. Everything rushed back at me at breakneck speed. I was in Roane's bed. His sheets were a welcoming cool touch against my naked skin and I turned to see him at his window, gazing outwards. His black pants rode low on his hips. There was no shirt in his hand this time, only worry in his eyes.

I swallowed tightly because I felt what he felt inside.

Resignation and fatigue. Underneath that was determination. He was going to win. He'd always known it and now it was time to remind everyone else.

"What'd you dream about?"

I curled against the headboard and wrapped the sheets around me. I felt exposed. "A lot of ramblings and crazy talk. There was a circus theme this time."

"Circus?" Roane frowned, but never moved away from the window.

The fairytale wasn't worth mentioning. "The Immortal told me that there was a snake charmer in my tent."

"You talk? You have conversations?" Roane looked taken aback.

"Yeah, anyway—the snake charmer sent a snake inside the tent."

He crossed to sit beside me on the bed. He sat with his back towards me and I watched the corded muscles on his back. He was primed and ready to go.

"I think... I'm the tent. The Immortal told me that, but someone was inside of me."

Roane swung his hypnotic eyes toward me.

I grinned and rasped out, "No, not you. She meant like an empath was inside of me. Sometimes... it's been known to happen. If an empath is skilled enough, they can find someone and look outward—look at where they're at. I did it. I had Blue do it to Kates for me."

"You think that someone was inside of you to see where you are?"

"I know it." The moment my eyes had opened, everything flooded to me. "Kates told me that Blue was in a coma. If I'd gone further inside of her I would've seen that Kates hadn't put Blue in a coma. She took her captive. Blue was being held in the same castle where they took me with Emily and Adam. I didn't search inside of her enough."

Roane stood and crossed to his closet. I watched as he flung open the doors and quickly rifled inside. "Tell me more." The command was thrown over his shoulder.

"Blue was inside my head. They made her go in when I had my shield down."

Roane paused and looked at me.

I swallowed painfully. "She got inside and they're coming here."

"That's what he intended the whole time." Roane suddenly stopped and straightened to his fullest height. Each muscle on his back stood out, primed and livid.

In that moment, I was suddenly aware of how Roane was a vampire. He was a predator and now he'd go against another predator. Roane was a Hunter. Their skills went unmatched by other vampires. It was why they were chosen to be the hunters of their own kind, but... Lucan was his human brother. And he led, what Kates believed to be, a revolution.

"They had no intention of you delivering a message to the Immortal. Let me guess, they have her boyfriend and they hoped she'd give herself up for him?"

I nodded. "How'd you know?"

"I can read thoughts. The girl they think is the Immortal has no idea what a shield is—and your shield was down too, Davy. I read that they'd taken Adam and Emily. I know that Kates used you."

"Did you read inside of my head what your brother really intends to do with the Immortal?"

Roane paused.

"He wants my blood because he wants his Family to have the Immortal's powers. He's hoping to have an army of unstoppable vampires so that they can reverse the decree. The one that states they can't hunt, bite, or kill humans. The one that started the Hunters in the first place and the one that'll allow Kates to do all the slaying she wants."

I looked at my hands, lifted them upwards, and gasped as I saw a glimpse of the sparkling diamond blood that I'd dreamt about. My eyes closed and then my normal skin was back. But I swore….

"No," Roane clipped out. "My brother doesn't just want to reverse the decree. My brother wants to rule the entire Vampire nation." He lifted his eyes once again to me. Then he reached inside his closet and pulled out a lethal sword. He strapped the sword diagonally across his back and lifted a gold necklace over his head. It hung on the apex of his chest. I wondered at the significance when I saw that a small leaf emblem that dangled from the chain.

"Well…," I searched for something to say. "At least he's ambitious."

Roane clipped out, "His 'ambition' just sealed his fate." Then his jaw clenched, unclenched, and clenched again. "He wants you. He can't have you."

CHAPTER TWENTY-THREE

Gregory came for me. He knocked once and announced his presence through the door.

"I'll… give me a second." I glanced around with a heavy head, drooped shoulders, and my heart was… not in my chest, but I moved my body as if it still belonged to me. Gregory knocked once more before I opened the door. "Okay. I'm ready."

He nodded with that same look in his eyes that I'd seen the first time. They were shrewd and he still looked at me in distaste, but I might've detected a small bit of sympathy. I wasn't sure. I was just happy that it wasn't Wren.

Gregory led me out. As we passed a circular stairwell in the middle of the hallway, I heard the buzz downstairs. The floor shook underneath my feet. The excitement in the air was addictive. I felt their thirst for blood. Every muscle in their bodies was stretched to the fullest from their anticipation.

A war was brewing.

As soon as we hit the outside air, something reeled inside of me. I felt another frenzy of excitement, rage, and carnal desire. Unlike inside, this frenzy was twice as bad. I looked out and saw one thing. I shouldn't have been able to see Roane, but I did. He stood on a hill, a dark figure among the shadows around him. He was a vampire and at that moment, I felt with confidence that he was the best.

There was no wind. The night was still, eerily so, but I felt the frenzy of activity from Roane's Family behind me. I felt it from the oncoming army too. Roane stood between the two armies and I wondered why he stood where he did.

As I got into the back seat, Gregory shut the door. As he slid beside me from the other side, I grasped his hand and shot inside before I realized what I had intended.

He wanted revenge. It was what he thirsted for, almost more than anything, but he'd been given an order. He intended to fulfill that order and I choked back tears as I heard Roane ordering him to protect me, keep me safe, and fulfill that duty above anything else. It cost Gregory, but he intended to see it through.

I almost shot back out of him, but I gritted my teeth and remembered my mistake with Kates. I looked further and saw the reason he wanted revenge. Raitscliff.

I remembered Roane's words. '*Raitscliff has vowed your death since Hartsdale.*'

Now I understood.

Raitscliff had turned Gregory's daughter. He sought revenge by murdering Raitscliff's second in command. Both vampires wanted the other's throat now.

I shuddered from the rage inside of Gregory, but I went further and got a rush of memories, emotions, and even worse, I heard his little girl. She laughed softly, delicately when he crooned as a proud father for her to sleep. They were both human in this memory. Then there was another memory where he held his arms out for her as she took her first steps.

She had golden curls and the warm brown eyes like her father. Then I saw when she'd been changed into a vampire for an enemy Family. As I started to pull out of him, I brushed against another thread of emotions. This one was his belief. He believed in Roane. He believed so fully, it brought tears to my eyes.

I gasped again and this time, I was inside of Roane. I saw through his eyes and felt inside his body. I felt his strength and fierce resolve. I didn't stop to wonder how I was inside of him, but I was. I stood on that hill, cloaked in darkness. I felt freed as an animal of the world, possibly the best.

Roane didn't relish his darkness. I felt a surge of sadness, but I didn't search through that. I couldn't, not yet. I looked out through his eyes. Unlike the dark reddish tint that I'd seen through Kates' eyes, his were crystal clear. His vision was magnified to make out a single droplet on a blade of grass. He saw everything.

He was chillingly patient as an army of vampires approached with the symbol of a lion painted on their bodies. They were on foot, silent and lethal. Their bodies weaved in and out of the shadows that were overcast from the woods surrounding Roane's home. They hoped for a surprise attack.

They failed.

He sniffed the air—Raitscliff. Roane took another long shuddering sniff and something pricked inside of him. There was no Lucan in the approaching army. Sixty beasts led by Raitscliff. He had forty behind him. The odds were favorable for the Roane Family.

"Get out of me, Davina!" Roane snarled and then shoved me out.

The car had pulled away, but I hadn't noticed. Gregory watched out the windows.

"What does Lucas intend to do?" My voice was scratchy.

Each muscle in his thick neck shifted until Gregory peered at me squarely. He had no idea that I'd been in there and that I knew what made him tick. "Lucas has a plan. He always has a plan. It should not matter to a human such as yourself."

I straightened in my seat. "I might be human, but I'm the reason all of this is happening. I don't care what you think of me. I care about what happens tonight. I want to know what Lucas is planning."

Gregory stared at me. "We both know what he plans."

Lucan's death.

"Lucan isn't back there. He's not going to Lucas' house. It's just Raitscliff—"

Gregory didn't move. He did nothing and yet, I felt his attention snap. It was now solely directed on me.

I continued with a dry mouth, "I… you know what I am." It wasn't the time to waste words. "You know what I can do. I was inside of you. I know what he did and I know what you did doesn't measure against what he did. It was wrong. I'm not a vampire. I don't understand you … people. To be honest, I don't care to ever understand, but I have a proposition…." Here we go—

"It's the luck of the Irish. Don't do it, yee lads."

I clasped my eyes close and cried out, "I'm not dreaming. There are rules. You can't invade my head now."

The Immortal laughed gaily. "I don't have to be lucky to be Irish. I'm the Immortal. I'm you, Davy. You've got the luck of a lass."

"Go away!"

"Now, now," it tsked me. "Ye caun't go tound screaming tah yaself. Peeple tink ya crazy, that's wat tey tink."

I glanced at Gregory. He thought I was crazy.

"You can't do this to him. You will not take away this man's last purpose."

I turned away and tried to whisper into my hand, "He's a vampire."

"The soul isn't kept in a neat locked box. The soul is imbedded into the body. The body remains and part of the soul still remains. He has a purpose. You will not tempt him and you will not remove that last purpose for his being."

Gregory had stilled.

I whispered back to the Immortal, "His purpose is to kill. That's what vampires do."

He growled deep in his throat. Then the Immortal lashed at me, "You are ignorant. That is unforgivable! His purpose is hope. He has hope in Roane, at what he believes Roane will achieve. You will take that away."

Huh?

"His daughter and enemy are his weaknesses. You will not take his hope by exploiting his weakness. You are not that type of person."

"I'm not a person."

"You are wrong. You are the last person I need."

Talk about hearing my own doom. I sighed and said instead to Gregory, "Can you just take me home?"

His big beefy hand jerked at my question. "Did you mean what you said? Is it really just Raitscliff back there?"

I jerked a shoulder up. "I lied. I wouldn't know that anyway." I wondered if he bought my lie and I, for once, had no idea what he wondered in return. A moment later he relaxed beside me. Then I heard the slight crunch of gravel beneath the tires and the wind against the window.

Absentmindedly, I noted, "The wind's picked up."

Gregory turned his thick neck. "I've known a few Immortals. It took them years, some lifetimes, before they could do what you've done in two days."

Something told me he hadn't bought my lie. I didn't reply back. What could I say?

'You're the last human I need.' The words haunted me and a fresh shiver crawled down my spine. I felt it all the way through my body and to my gut. Something didn't bode well for me… but I'd have to figure it out later. A war was about to break out and I knew that I needed to do something about it. I had to stop it, but I had no idea how to do that. Pre-Immortal age, I would've sought out Blue… .and then the light bulb turned on. Blue was awake. Blue was not in a coma. And I could talk to Blue—but not in the physical sense.

"Stupid!" I should've thought of that before.

Gregory didn't spare me a look. It was a good feeling. We had become acclimated to each other.

I closed my eyes, hunkered down, and sought out Blue. It only took a second before I found myself in her head. She was not so blue, though. She was furious and seeing red wherever she looked. Her arms were jerking in rhythm, scraping away at something, and her teeth were gritted. Then I remembered that Blue wasn't a vampire. I couldn't communicate with her.

'They can't know about Davy. I can't tell them.'

I sucked in a panicked breath.

'Jacith sent me for a reason. I can't let them know Davy's the one.' Blue continued, *'I told them Lucas' position. He can handle them. Everything is not lost. They still think the other girl is the Immortal. Everything is still safe. They cannot be divided.'*

How did Blue know? What did Blue know? What did she mean when she said we couldn't be divided? We already were.

Before I pulled completely out of Blue, I heard a different voice from inside of her. It was deep, ominous, and I almost felt the immortality from it. *'He will need her at the end otherwise all will be lost.'*

The deep voice sent shivers down my spine and something took root inside of me. I needed to be there, at whatever it was. I needed to be beside Roane. With that thought, the decision took over my body. I looked down and watched as my body turned into a glowing beacon. I was faintly aware of Gregory's jerk in reaction.

The Immortal was taking over.

I swallowed tightly as I didn't know if I wanted it or if I was just along for the ride. Either way, I closed my eyes tightly, and knew the next second would decide my fate.

CHAPTER TWENTY-FOUR

Something burst inside of me and I felt my body shoot into the air. Gregory twisted around me like I was in the eye of a tornado. He was quickly replaced with the car, the surrounding road, and the other cars. I was in the air and everything started to circle around me. Looking down, I saw the Raitscliff Family beneath my feet. I could barely make out the symbol of the lion until they suddenly started to circle so fast it was a constant blur. It was like a colorful wall and I gasped when a lion burst out of the blurred wall. It lifted its head and let loose with a deafening roar. It closed its massive mouth and then hung its head before it vanished.

For the first time in my sanity, I reached out for the Immortal. "Please stop this. I mean it! I can't—I just want this to stop. Please stop."

And for the first time, the Immortal didn't answer.

I closed my eyes and felt my body slam to the ground. My legs were unsteady, but I looked up to see the surrealness around me. Kates and Lucan stood in front of me. I squeaked in panic, but when they didn't react, I relaxed slightly.

Lucan was in the front, perfectly straight and with confidence in his shoulders. His black eyes were intense as he looked at something in the distance. He thirsted for what he thought was next to come. His jaw was clenched tight. I watched, horrified, as his nostrils slowly flared. It was like he smelled blood in the air. Then I saw patches of his skin break out to form a puzzle. He was the puzzle, but the pieces were off. It was like something had been put together wrong.

Kates stood with her head half bent towards the ground and a hand outstretched to touch the back of his. An air of intimacy swirled around them. But while he stood with no regrets, I saw a shadow in Kates. Her hair had slipped down her cheek and lifted in the air. It moved slowly, so slowly. I realized that time still moved forward, but crawled at a snail's pace. Not me.

'There are rules, universal laws of nature stuff and... The Immortals are able to bend those rules.'

I was bending time—no. The Immortal was bending time or... I was. It didn't matter who was doing it because it was happening. Then I saw Kates bite the corner of her lip. If I'd been any other person, I wouldn't have caught that gesture. She was having second thoughts—and something else flooded inside of me. There was still something in her that knew her path was wrong. Hope flared in me.

Then something else exploded inside of me and I was hurtled through the same tornado of time as before. When I stopped again, I saw Shelly huddled in a far corner. She was pale and tears were frozen in midair on her cheek. Wren grasped her shoulder tightly. The two looked in complete contrast with Shelly's yellow sweater and Wren's hooker outfit. Then something prickled the back of my neck and I turned around.

Roane stared directly at me. His eyelid twitched and I almost screamed when he hurled himself at me. When Roane's hand touched my arm, I was thrown out of my time-loop thing. It felt like we both tumbled out of invisible glue and fell roughly against the opposite wall.

Wren and Shelly both jumped, but Roane pressed against me. "What the hell are you doing here?"

I couldn't really tell him that it was a deep and foreboding voice inside of Blue's head that sent me to him. In fact, I couldn't even explain how I'd gotten to him, but I had.

"Are we in your restaurant? Weren't you just outside of your place?" There were three tables set up in a corner. Diamond-encrusted glasses sat on top of them. I recognized those glasses. They were from the Alexander Restaurant.

"I'm every girl's best friend," I said faintly, echoing the Immortal's words.

Roane frowned fiercely, but pressed closer. He shifted and blocked me from Shelly and Wren. I wasn't even sure if Shelly knew I was there. It had all happened so fast, but I figured that Wren could smell me.

"I sent you with Gregory." He was enraged. A shiver passed through me—it was one of those sorts that I always got around him. What was it about this guy?—vampire. What was it about this vampire? My legs forgot they had bone in them whenever he was in the vicinity.

I needed to be distracted. "I zapped away from him. Don't worry. You can't blame him. He couldn't stop me... and how could you? That's annoying."

Roane replied swiftly, "You drank my blood. I'm connected to you."

I wasn't sure if I was comfortable with that thought.

"You didn't answer me. Why are you here?" Roane pressed.

I looked towards one of the walls, the north wall, and I felt what was on the other side. "He's here. He's out there. And he knows that you're in here."

Roane followed my gaze, but he never questioned what I said. "How far?"

"Across the road. Kates is with him."

Roane narrowed his eyes and quickly crossed to a window. As he moved away, the cold replaced his warmth.

Shelly gasped in surprise. "Davy? What are you—How? Oh thank god!"

I attempted a smile, but just sighed in the end. She shouldn't have been grateful to see me. I was the reason she was there and yet—I couldn't not appreciate the irony. Shelly Witless was happy to see me. Only the supernatural could do something like that.

Shelly frowned, confused. When she moved toward me, Wren held her back. "Wha—Davy... are you... do you know these people?"

There it was again, just like Emily and Adam. All three of them thought they were held captive by people. If only it were true. I didn't say anything. What could I say?

Roane moved away from the window. "They've got us surrounded."

Wren growled. "How many?"

"Lucan's army. They split up."

"Our Family?"

"We should be okay." Roane hauled me behind him as he strode through the door. I heard Shelly cry out and knew Wren did the same with her. He led the way down a narrow hallway and out onto a slight perch. We were on a third floor that I hadn't known existed in the restaurant. I glanced down and saw the fountain in the middle of the room. Our table must've been right underneath where we stood now, but I hadn't had time to study the restaurant's interior before.

I studied it now and saw that the fountain was larger than I thought. Giant goldfish circled in the clear blue water. Then I looked at the bottom and blinked twice before I realized that there was no bottom. The fountain fell to a depth that I couldn't see. I glanced at Roane and briefly thought about slipping inside. His eyes could see it.

"Don't even think it."

"How do you do that?" It was becoming annoying. I had my shield up, with the little bit of effort that I needed now, but it was up. He could still read my mind.

"I don't have to be a genius to know what you were thinking," Roane muttered before he turned and swept us down a narrow stairway to our left. I said swept, but we really flew downwards. It only took a second before our feet landed with a swoosh on the main floor.

I heard another swoosh behind us.

"Oh—!"

"We're going underground?" Wren's voice was tightly restrained.

I looked over my shoulder and gulped when her eyes landed on me. She hated me. I saw it. But she was like Gregory. She followed Roane. She believed in him. And for the second time, I wondered what vampire could inspire loyalty like that.

She growled a warning and Roane jerked me in front of him. His hand fell from my arm and planted itself on my waist. He steered me in front of him and answered Wren at the same time, "Yes, we'll go underground. A tunnel connects to the mansion. We can regroup and head out of town."

"We're running." I heard the distaste in her voice.

"No." Roane stopped and looked behind. He stared her down. "We are being smart. There are two armies to our one. Right now, we have an entire army behind us."

"It's a Family," Wren retorted.

"Yes, a Family of vampires. It's an army to our two, Wren. I won't chance it."

"Vampires!" Shelly squeaked. I heard another cry of pain a moment later and knew Wren must've tightened her hold.

Wren bit out, "You wanted to send the replacement away. I understood that, but I knew you were going to come and fight. Now we're running. You would've chanced it if she hadn't shown up."

Oh—we all knew who she meant.

Roane had already been stiff before, but now he was like cement. My finger twitched. I fought against the urge to trail it down his arm, just to feel him. It wasn't the time or place.

I closed my eyes and mentally repeated that to myself. I'd said it a third time when I felt Wren back down from Roane. I didn't know what he'd said, but it must've worked. I felt the surrender in the air and then Roane turned to steer me forward again.

He wasn't as rigid as before. I wondered if he knew what

had passed through my mind when I felt one of his fingers dip underneath my waistband and started to rub back and forth.

My legs started to turn into jelly and I leaned back against him once before he realized what was happening. He chuckled underneath his breath, for my ears only, and removed his hand.

I bit my lip to keep from crying out in protest, but it was the right thing to do. An army was coming and we were on the run. It was definitely not the time for my legs to melt into the ground.

Roane directed me around the main floor, through a myriad of tables. As we passed the fountain, I glanced down again and caught a swish of a tail from the deeper depths.

"Focus, Davy," Roane murmured into my ear. "We'll be fine."

"She will be. She can't die, but the rest of us can," Wren snarled. I heard the swift swish of her leather as she strode behind us.

Roane steered us to a back door and as his hand reached out, glass shattered behind us. He stopped, but I watched in fascination as his hand flexed momentarily. He fought against an urge and then decided something as he turned slowly…. My heart was effectively in my throat. I tried to peak around him, but Roane kept me in place behind him.

Wren growled. I jumped when I heard another deeper undertone that she hadn't added before. It had been from Wren before, but this sound was from the vampire.

All the sudden, Shelly and Wren moved away. Shelly screamed in protest and Roane's hand slipped behind me. He grabbed the doorknob, but didn't turn it. I watched, confused, and then as another explosion occurred, Roane pushed the door open. I was quickly on the other side before I realized what happened and the door was shut behind me.

Well… hell.

I turned and looked at the closed door. Roane didn't want me in danger. I got that, but what he didn't know is that we couldn't be divided—for whatever reason. The scary voice inside of Blue's head said so.

I heard another explosion on the other side followed by a loud thump. I pressed my ear against the door and heard a lot of growling, a bunch more thumps. When I heard a shrill scream, the pain blasted me. I could've blocked it, but I didn't want to—I sighed in relief when I realized it wasn't Roane. Then I slipped inside their pain and nearly choked as they died. The body's coldness quickly became cemented. It had been a vampire, but now it was just a body. His eyes were open. I looked through him at the room from the ground. His head was turned to the right and I had a perfect view of the action.

Wren had shoved Shelly into a corner with a table to block her.

Roane warned me never to be alone with her. Now I knew why.

She swept forward, dodged a vampire, grabbed his leg and another's leg and rolled to the ground. She used her body's momentum and both vampires fell to the ground. Their necks snapped as she completed her roll. Somehow, she grabbed a knife in each hand and quickly stuck them into two more vampires who were focused on Roane.

My mouth went dry watching her. All of the sudden, I felt another searing pain in my chest. I gasped and clutched my chest. When I pulled it away, I was surprised to find there was no blood. I'd expected blood and then I cursed underneath my breath. I quickly slipped back into the dead vampire and looked for Roane. I couldn't see him. The pain must've been his.

When I tried to get inside of Roane, he lashed at me, *'Stay out!'*

I tried again—nothing. Roane had completely locked me out.

The dead vampire was turned the other way now. He wasn't a help and so I did what I probably shouldn't have. I slipped inside of Wren. She was boiling with adrenalin, excitement, and wrath all at once. Complicated.

As she bent forward, I reeled, and suddenly she was back up with her legs in the air and her fists between them. I felt like I was on a roller coaster. Then another scream punctured the air and everything froze.

Wren whirled around, her insides surging.

Lucan held Shelly in front of him with his mouth turned towards her neck. He lowered his teeth, but looked up—Wren followed the gaze—and there stood Roane with two vampires in his hands.

It was a direct challenge.

Roane straightened, deftly flexed his hands and snapped the vampires' necks. Their bodies fell to the ground and he stepped over them, calm and assured.

Wren stretched her hands, ready for Roane's command. None came. He held his human brother's gaze steadily. "Do you want to drink? Go ahead. You know what will happen."

Lucan grinned, lethally, and nipped lightly at Shelly's skin.

She shuddered against his chest, but Lucan only had eyes for Roane. "Is this how you thought it'd end? After all this time and I've got the girl in my arms. You had your chance, brother. Too bad you forgot who you were when you went to them."

"Do you want the Immortal or do you want me?" Roane threw out the challenge.

CHAPTER TWENTY-FIVE

For a moment I saw indecision in Lucan's eyes. Roane was right. Lucan did want his brother back, but something had gone wrong between them, more than the ready-to-kill-each-other type of wrong. "Is that what it would take, Lucas? If I let her go, would you remember who you're supposed to be? Do you think I'm *still* the stupid one?" A hard glint appeared in Lucan's black eyes. "Or maybe if I drink from her, you'll have no other choice. You'll have to come back to my side."

"That's what you want, isn't it?"

I felt Roane's confidence. It was sweltering, sexy, and entirely too alarming. I felt what was on the other side—the acceptance of what was to come….

Lucan hesitated, but an emotion quickly stormed in those blackened eyes. His hand grasped Shelly's neck tighter and a vein jerked in her neck.

Wren wetted her lips. She wanted a taste too, but her fear and loyalty to Roane held her back.

For a moment, just a moment, I was tempted to slip inside of Shelly, but I knew the fear would paralyze me. I didn't know for sure if I could withstand it, but then another thought came to my mind….With a gasp, I was inside of Shelly. The terror was suffocating, but I tried to wade through it. It was like hardening cement. I felt Lucan pressed behind me. I felt my neck, Shelly's neck, trembling and weak. Then a box opened behind me. There was a light, but it quickly shut off.

The terror was gone. The trembling had stopped. Shelly had gone into a back corner of her mind where she could escape. She was no longer in control of her body. I would've done the same thing. Hell, I *had* done the same thing in my recent past.

Then I slipped into every pore of her body. Lucan stilled at the sudden change, but then Shelly's body jerked when I took control. He continued, "You had your chance, brother. You could've been beside me through eternity. You chose the wrong side. I've got her now and I'll reign in your defeat."

My eyes—Shelly's eyes—snapped to Roane. His eyes narrowed as he sensed the change. He paused, studied me/Shelly, and comprehension flared in his eyes. He looked towards the closed door where my body stood, but swung back to Shelly.

He knew—and he was pissed.

Roane chose his words carefully. "You need to be careful, Lucan. Things aren't as they seem. Things are… undecided."

Wren frowned and glanced to her leader.

Roane took a purposeful step forward. He didn't step forward, he stalked forward.

Lucan stilled—I wasn't inside of him, but I felt his body's answer to the sudden shift in Roane's body. Roane had been cautious, held himself back before and now there was no holding back. Lucan registered it all and I wondered how long it would be before he realized who exactly he held in his arms. It wasn't my body. It wasn't my blood, but I still didn't want to feel his fangs rip through Shelly's skin.

"What's undecided, brother?" Lucan enjoyed the back and forth. "You led with me. You were the one who had this grand idea. It was just because she was a child. That's the only reason why you stopped. You're weak. You were weak then and you're weak now. You protect her even though this one means nothing to you."

Roane's attention snapped to his brother. For the first time since the battle had started, Roane wasn't focused on me. I frowned as I wondered who Lucan referred to….

He sounded malicious. "You hunted the first one. You were supposed to have the first drink. It shouldn't have meant anything that the thread jumped to her child."

"Shut up, Lucan!" Roane growled.

"It's the truth. And the thread's not in Talia anymore. Your lover died. You weren't even there to protect her. That's what you had chosen. You chose her over me." Disdain and bitterness dripped from Lucan, but I watched horrified as something glazed over Roane's eyes at the words.

Her? Lover?

Roane and Talia, the previous Immortal, had been lovers. From the clenched jaw, I judged that he still loved her…. I closed my eyes tightly as tears stung them. They were a knee jerk reaction.

Lucan continued, "You fell in love with a child. Only a vampire can be that sick, but I understood. I did, Lucas. I'm your brother. I understand things like love at first sight. You fought me for her, but that's over. She's not alive anymore. You can forget this charade and take up my side again. I need my brother beside me. It hasn't been the same without you."

"I didn't fall in love with Talia until she was an adult. I fought you that day because she was a child. We don't hurt children."

"Yes, we do. We're vampires. Why do you keep denying what we are?"

I opened my eyes, Shelly's eyes, a crack and glimpsed the pain in Roane through her tears—my tears that her body produced from my suffering.

Roane shook his head. "I'm no longer your brother, Lucan. That ceased when Jaleathus sired me. The Roane's Family blood became mine. We live with different standards in our blood."

Lucan snorted in contempt. "Don't tell me about your different standards. They come from Jacith. He brainwashed your entire Family, but you're still vampires. You try to pretend you aren't. I'm *insulted* that they did this to my brother."

A bitter laugh wrung out of Roane. "You were nothing without me, Lucan. I told you how to act. I told you how to think. I told you everything. You wouldn't have done anything if I hadn't been there."

Lucan froze behind me. I felt rage build inside of him. His fingers tightened on Shelly's throat. His other hand gripped her arm until I felt a trickle of blood seep downwards. It trickled over his hands, but he didn't realize it. Roane's nostrils flared at the smell. So did Wren's. I glanced around the room. All of them except Wren and Roane eyed the blood. It was Immortal blood... or so they thought.

"You're wrong," Lucan whispered. "I lead my Family. I've found the Immortal. I have her in my arms. You failed, brother."

Roane smiled. It was a confident, too smooth, type of smile. Lucan gripped harder on Shelly's arm—more blood slipped downwards. It trickled over her palm, down her finger, and hung just off the tip of the nail.... My heart pounded heavily as I waited... then it let loose and splattered on the floor.

Still no reaction from Lucan.

He was focused, almost crazily focused on Roane. "Now what is your Family going to do? You were supposed to protect the Immortal and you couldn't do that, could you?"

"I'm a Hunter, Lucan. Are you forgetting what that means? I'm connected to all of the other Hunters. You rip into that girl and I can call on them. You won't be fighting just me. You'll be fighting all of them."

"I'll have the Immortal's blood. I'll be unstoppable." Lucan was so sure, so confident in his own words. I knew instantly when he smelled the blood. His body jerked in reaction and I/Shelly was slammed against a wall. His fangs clamped onto Shelly's neck and sunk further. He drank—oh—I fought against it. The blood was pulled out at breathtaking speed. I couldn't... I tried to slow the draining, but it was useless.

Lucan was a starved animal. Shelly whimpered from inside of her box. She felt her body's death. I saw the box open and the light shone briefly before she crawled out of the box. There she was, terrified, but calm. She knew her death was almost there.

I almost wished that Shelly had been a vampire. I could've talked to her, comforted her in that moment, but she wasn't. She was just a human, but it was a good thing that Shelly was a human. Life was simple for her.

I felt her heart slowing… thump… thump… she closed her eyes and fell. Her heart had stopped. Lucan let go, confused, and Shelly's body really did fall to the ground.

"She's dead," he muttered, stricken. "But…"

Kates had been silent the entire time. She gasped now, "It's not her. She's not the Immortal, but—"

I could still hear from Shelly's body, but I couldn't see anything anymore. I didn't want to stay inside of her and then I heard Kates again. "Lucan, what do we do?" Panic trembled just on the tip of her tongue, but I wondered where that had come from. Kates never panicked. I left Shelly and found Kates easily.

'It can't be, but I wonder… it can't be,' Kates thought. I caught an image of myself and knew my nolstage was connecting dots faster than I was comfortable with.

'You can't, there's no way. You never could before…'

Kates knew I'd been on the roof with Talia. She'd known that Talia was the Immortal.

'She's the empath that was cozying up with The Hunter.'

Kates had been surprised when I'd shown up at the Shoilster with Roane… now it was starting to make sense.

'She's the Immortal.' Kates cursed to herself.

I slipped out of Kates before I felt whatever she was feeling now. I shouldn't have. I should've stayed inside of her because I knew my nolstage had power over Lucan—therefore over my livelihood, but I was a coward. I drew in another shuddering breath as I opened my own eyes and stared at the same door. I lifted a hand and tentatively touched the wood with my palm. It was so sturdy, but just on the other side… everything was barely hanging in the balance.

'Your lover died.'

I pressed a knuckled fist against my mouth. Talia and Roane had been lovers. He had loved her. I remembered the stricken expression in Roane's eyes as Lucan had said those words. It had been pure love, the kind that was meant for the rest of a lifetime. He had loved someone else like that… and me… I realized that there had been nothing between us.

My stomach turned over suddenly. I could've thrown up in that moment. I glanced downwards, distantly, as I looked at my stomach. Roane was drawn to the Immortal inside of me. A part of Talia was inside of me. He was drawn to her. He needed her—not me. I was just the body.

'Davy,' Roane called to me with his thoughts.

I jerked my head to the side. I didn't want to talk to him, not at that moment, but it was irrational. I didn't want to deal with what was really happening on the other side of that door. He had no obligation to me. We'd only… we'd only been together one time.

Just once.

That was it. Right? There had been no words of affection, no… no nothing. He had loved her. How was I supposed to compete with that? I couldn't. The answer was so bleak to me, but still….

'Davy!' Roane was more urgent this time. 'Davy, you need to get out of here. There's a hallway that goes down. Follow it, keep going. You'll pass the fountain below us. Keep going. You need to get out of here, away from Lucan. He knows it's not Shelly. It's only a matter of time before he figures it out. He's already looking at the door. You have to hurry.'

It hurt to even hear his voice. 'Kates knows. She figured it out.'

There was a pause. 'Yeah. I can see that. You have to hurry, Davy. The tunnel will go all the way to the mansion. It should be safe by the time you get there. Find Gregory.'

I was supposed to run. My childhood best friend, my vampire—I didn't know what Roane was—and so many others were in the room behind me. Shelly was dead. I knew I wouldn't die. I was the

Immortal and I had a strong feeling the thread wasn't going to jump to anyone else—if it did then I was dead anyway.

I was stuck.

Run, not run, hide, not hide. What could I do? I knew what I wanted to do. I always ran. I pressed sweating palms to my pants and tried to wipe them off. I turned, faltering, and stared at where Roane urged me to go. The tunnel was dark, but it didn't seem ominous. The room behind me was too ominous, but the sound of the water calmed me slightly. It ran through the wall beside my ear. Before I knew what I was doing, my foot had stretched outwards and I found myself slowly passing through the darkness.

I kept going and the water grew louder.

The tunnel dipped forward. I felt gravity on my body and knew I was heading downwards.

I took a harsh breath and clasped my eyes tightly together. I needed to be honest with myself. I was escaping. It wasn't because Roane told me to go. He loved someone else, someone that was inside of me now. That hurt—it seared deep down, almost too far for my empathic abilities to comprehend. Well, that's not true. I could comprehend it, I just didn't want to. I wanted to run from it. He was behind me. Kates was in that room. She had the knowledge to change my life forever. I could be hunted if Lucan found out who I was.

I stopped in the tunnel and drew in a ragged breath.

I could go back, but to what? Why? Lucan wanted my powers. He couldn't have them. I knew that no matter the odds, Roane would best his brother. What was I afraid of? I could run... there was no danger.

But... I remembered the voice inside of Blue's head. Roane and I could not be separated.

"Are we on a pity party? Is this what the staggering amount of suffering and confliction is about?" The Immortal chose to announce its presence.

I sighed in contempt. "Now is not the time. Why can I hear you like you're here?"

"I'm the Immortal. Have you forgotten our first trip around the merry go round? You're the pail. What do you carry? Who are Jack and Jill? You should know this by now!"

"Stop it—"

"—THINK!" The Immortal screamed. "Who's Jack and Jill? You are the Immortal! You think I was the one pulling all those strings back there where you catapulted yourself out of that car and behind your sidekick? I didn't do that, Davy. I wasn't the one in the drivers' seat. That was all you. I was riding shotgun. You were the Immortal. You, not me, not this voice you keep hearing. It was all you."

My throat went dry at those words. The thread was inside of me. The thread jumped from person to person, body to body. I wasn't—there was no way, but everyone had been shocked by the speed my body had acclimated to the Immortal thread. Gregory said some took years to do what I'd done in two days, but none of it made sense. What did it mean that I had done what I had? If it hadn't been the Immortal… it was me? Who was I?

"Cut out the Buddha bull. You can ponder the eternal question of your identity later. You've got to stop moaning in your own piss and get back to that room."

"Are you my conscious? Are you the good angel now?"

"That's the issue, honey bunny. I'm neither. I'm the in between. I'm the go between. I'm the reason that your devil is on the left and the angel is on the right. That's me—that's you now so you better start deciphering it!"

The Immortal was pissing me off. "Get out of me!"

She chuckled. "Are you angry? You're more than clueless. You're choosing your ignorance. You can't walk away when you know you're needed in that other room."

"Shut up! I don't care. I'm doing what Roane wants."

The Immortal laughed. "You're doing what you want. You're running away because you got your feelings hurt. You're being a sissy. The boy likes someone that's not you. Boo freaking hoo. Wake up! You're more than that and all that romance crap is nothing compared to what's going to happen if you don't get your butt back there. Stop feeling with your emotions and think with your head."

I was empathic. Feelings *were* my thing.

"Well, they aren't anymore," the Immortal snapped. "You want to know a little about yourself? A long *long* time ago a visionary realized what vampires could do. He saw how dangerous they could be so he went and created a 'prophecy' that said one day, a person who was interwoven with the essence of life would take *their* life from them. You're feared by vampires, but also desired. Some think you were created as an ultimate weapon against them, but then rumors started going around that they could drink from you. If they drank your blood, they could get your powers. That's the prophecy, Davy. The prophecy *was* created and the Immortal thread came to be. You've got the essence of life flowing through every particle of your body. All the other girls, yes—even Talia—they weren't the Immortal. They were just the carriers for the thread. One would come and become the Immortal. That's you—not them. And if you want to sit and mope that Roane loves Talia, someone who was less than you, you disgust me."

As shocking revelations came… this one was big.

It continued, "Every vampire out there thinks they can drink from you and they'll have your powers. That's what they've been taught. You're the toad to their Cinderella. They're wrong. If they'd bitten any other carrier then they would've gotten the powers. The thread would've jumped to them, given them a flare of power, but immediately attached itself to the first human they would've touched. No vampire can handle the essence of life inside of them. It goes against their grain as a vampire. They thrive on pain. They thrive on suffering, on darkness, on death. We are the light. We are life. You are life, Davy, and you're the prophecy."

All this now… how could this help now?

"It'll help because you know something they don't. The prophecy states that when the Immortal becomes one, instead of giving them powers, you will give them life. You'll strip them of their immortality, Davy."

"They'll be human?"

"You'll make their heart beat. Again."

The answer was so quaint.

"But what about Blue? What the voice inside her head said? Roane and I aren't supposed to be divided?" I'd been running when I knew that the ancient voice had commanded otherwise. I should be ashamed.

"That was Jacith. He's a moron who believes he's got way more power than he does. You have that power now. Not him. You have the knowledge. Not him, but you are needed back there. Get back there! NOW!"

The decision slammed into my chest.

The sound of water tickled behind the back of my head. I focused on it again. It was louder than before. Roane had said the tunnel would pass the fountain. Maybe…I moved forward and as the water grew louder, I knew what I needed to do. Determination rang through me when I felt the tunnel dip dramatically below my feet and the sound of rushing water slammed against my ears.

A rock wall was beside me. It was dank to the touch and I closed my eyes because I could feel the water on the other side. It was swirling angrily, ferocious to hear. When I'd been upstairs, I had tried to look for the bottom of the fountain. I hadn't been able to see it, but now I wondered if I was nearing the end. I pressed further and the sound grew louder and louder.

The water slammed against the rock. As I turned a corner, there it was. I'd come to an opening in the tunnel. The water rushed past me and dramatically turned to the left, but not before some of it splashed over a small hedge that separated the water from the tunnel. It disappeared from there, but there was a small walking path beside the water.

I watched the water, saw deep into the blue depths, and before I knew it—I had raised my hand above the water. Something sparked inside of me and I watched from outside my body. The water lifted out of the fountain and held still in the air. It waited for my hand's command, my command.

I had no idea if I was doing it or the Immortal, but I held my breath as I raised my hand. The water followed. It lifted from the floor before I settled it back down, gently. That's when I stepped on top of the hedge and before I knew it, I'd stepped on top of the water. A part of me screamed inside, but I watched my face from outside my body. I looked calm, in control, and confident.

She knew what she was doing. She knew where she was going. She was secure. Then the water rose around her and shot upwards.

CHAPTER TWENTY-SIX

I watched from a distance as my body rode that water upwards. It surged, rolled, and seemed to thunder as gravity was flipped upside down. I couldn't take my eyes off of myself. Something totally alien took over my body. My normally frizzy brown curls were sleek as they lay against my shoulders. The curls perfectly framed my face and my lips seemed to form a small heart.

As we—me and myself—neared the top, I watched my eyelids lift and I froze in shock.

I had brown eyes, but they were silver. They seemed to see everything at once. Then they turned towards me and seemed to zap me. "Get back. Now!"

I felt myself sucked through the air and crashed into my body. I gasped, choked, and struggled against what was happening.

"Accept me. Accept yourself," The Immortal me told myself. This voice was me. I wondered, belatedly, if I could have three different personas inside of me and still be sane. Maybe. I doubted it, though.

"Accept—now!" With that last command, I threw back my head, my arms jerked upwards, and I gasped as something flowed down my throat. It molded to my body. Then the world rushed at me with breakneck speed. I lifted high and over. The water fell away and I looked around the room.

Kates was frozen beside Lucan. Her blue eyes were wide, terrified, but what drew my eye wasn't how she looked at me. It was the knowledge that burned bright. She'd known, but seeing it was a different matter. Still… that wasn't the knowledge that I saw. She knew something else was going to happen, something that she didn't want to admit to herself. I saw it so bright. It was like a candle that flickered behind her.

"You!" Lucan growled. His hair was pushed back, carelessly, but it molded to the sides of his face. His eyes gleamed cruelly and he sneered as if knowing he'd won.

I felt Roane jerk forward. He stepped to move between myself and his brother, but I stopped him. When I lifted a hand, the room rattled. "No."

"Wha—" Kates gasped and jerked her head around.

"Holy fu—." Even Wren was amazed as she took in the scene.

"Davy, stop," Roane said, but it was too late.

I moved around and stepped in front of Lucan. As I looked down at him, I realized that I was floating in the air. Something prickled the back of my wrist and I looked around.

Every glass, every champagne flute, every crystal dish floated in the air. All those diamonds sparkled furiously. They were blinding, but I saw them through my silver eyes. They looked like air particles to me.

"What—you're the Immortal. You!" Lucan took a step forward.

"Lucan!" Roane shouted a warning.

I spoke above Roane. "Yes. I am she. I am the Immortal."

My voice was different. It wasn't just mine, but all the Immortals before me. Something ancient poured through me. It was frightening, but I felt the power. "I am not what you want, Lucan. That is my only warning."

"Davy, don't do this," Kates whispered this time. "Please. Please don't do this."

I merely looked at her. The candle started to burn brighter.

Lucan growled ferociously this time. He reached for my wrist, but two things happened in the blink of my eye. Kates stepped in front of him, her back to me. And Roane flung himself forward.

I stopped everything.

Time stood still, but Roane jerked me behind him. As I fell to the floor, I raised my head. "That's right. You're connected to me."

"My blood is in you." Roane turned and glared at his brother.

"He's frozen. I stopped time."

"So I see," Roane breathed harshly. He raked a chilling glare over his brother again before he turned and regarded me.

I stood to meet him and tilted my chin for respect. "You don't approve of what I've done."

"This isn't you, Davy. This is the Immortal. You're not…" He gestured to my body. "This isn't you. I want you back."

I could've told him that this was the new me, but instead I stepped around him. I stared at Kates and breathed out in awe, "Look at her."

The candle now shone brightly behind her. The blinding yellow flame encompassed her body. She was a mere black shadow in front of it.

"Do you see it?" I wanted him to see it.

Roane frowned, but looked. "It's the slayer. She's trying to save Lucan."

She wasn't. She wasn't doing that at all. My hand rose of its own volition, but it dropped now, saddened. "You don't see it."

"She doesn't want me to hurt him. She's in love with him, what do you expect?"

"She's not saving him. She thinks she's saving me. It's so bright around her. It's her hope." The candle burned even brighter now. It looked like it was going to explode. "She's saving herself."

"She's not, Davy." Roane was firm. "Kates is smart. She knows that I wouldn't let him touch you. She's making her move against me, not for you."

He was wrong. Roane didn't realize what had happened. He didn't really understand who I was anymore. Everything he knew was limited. All the vampires thought wrong.

It didn't matter, not right then, but I turned and gazed at my lover. He looked fierce with murder in his eyes. Every part of him screamed that he was an animal, but I remembered what he'd said before.

"There's a soul inside of you."

Roane frowned, jerked off balance for a moment.

I moved forward and lifted a palm to his chest. His muscles jerked in response from my touch, but he held still.

I continued, "You told me before that you don't have a soul, but your body remembers what it did with the soul. That's why you breathe sometimes. The soul is imbedded in every part of a person. You're still a person. You still have a soul. And you honor it, even now when you want to kill your brother."

'He cannot divide them.'

I understood them now. I glanced over my shoulder at Lucan. "He's not put together right. I saw that before, but I didn't understand it. I knew you'd win today. I felt your strength. What you said was right. You have the strength of all the Hunters inside of you. You'd overpower your brother too easily, but that's where it'd rip away your humanity. You'd become the animal that you loathe inside of you."

Roane stiffened at my words. He started to pull away, but I clasped the back of his arm. I wouldn't let him move and his eyes widened at my strength. "If you had killed your brother today, that would've destroyed you. He's still a part of you. You love him and you'd be the end of him. It would've been the end of you as well. I can't have that. I need you."

His eyes clung to mine.

I touched his lips. They were perfect, cool to the touch, and I leaned forward to nip at them.

Roane grasped the back of my head and deepened the kiss. I felt his love with that kiss, but I pulled away. Haunted. "Do you love me or do you love who is inside of me?"

His eyes shuddered closed and he withdrew. "I loved her, yes."

"That's why you're drawn to me."

"That's why you're drawn to me too!" Roane whipped back to me. I was taken aback by the loathing in his eyes. "You don't think

I've thought of this? Something takes control of you when you're around me. It's not you, either, Davy. You might think you feel something for me, but you don't. A part of Talia is inside of you. It's always her reaching out for me, taking control of you."

Oh god. I didn't… I couldn't understand… I started to slip inside of him, but he shoved me out. "I don't want you to know the mess inside of me."

I respected his wish. I couldn't solve the problem between us, but I knew a problem that I *could* resolve for him. So I looked back at Lucan. "You can't help your brother, but I can."

"Wha—"

I rushed forward and stepped in front of Kates. My back was to Lucan. And then I unlocked time.

"No!" Roane shouted, but I snapped my fingers. Every glass, every diamond, every champagne flute exploded in the air. They all ducked from the exploding shards of glass.

I whispered to Lucan, "I want to give you what you want."

He licked his fangs and grasped my arm. That was all he needed and he jerked me forward to clamp onto my skin. I tensed as my skin broke underneath his fangs, but I grasped his head. I willed him to drink all he needed.

"No!" Roane leapt across the room and pulled his brother from me. Lucan fell against a wall, bewildered and triumphant. Then his back arched dramatically. Only his head and toes touched the floor. He sucked in a ragged breath and pounded at his chest frantically. Desperate.

Roane stopped in front of me. He held me back with an arm around my waist and watched in confusion. "What?"

I watched Roane as he watched his brother. "He can be right again. I saved your brother… for you."

"What did you do, Davy?" The words were wrung out from him. Roane stared as Lucan howled in pain and rolled on the ground.

My words were for his ears only. "I gave him life again. He can be right."

Lucan continued to writhe on the floor, but Roane suppressed a shudder and abruptly turned so he couldn't watch anymore. He pulled me tight against his chest and wrapped both his arms around me. He buried his head in the crook of my shoulder and I watched for him. One of my hands lifted to cradle the back of his head.

Everyone watched in the room. No one dared to speak. Then Lucan's body lifted off the floor, his back arched, and a dark light ripped out of his mouth. It slammed to the ceiling and settled there. Waiting. I'd kept the crystals floating in the air and now I turned my wrist. Each little shattered particle of crystal all moved as one.

"Be gone," I whispered.

Immediately the crystals surrounded the black light and an explosion occurred.

Roane jerked. Everyone gasped. Kates fell to the floor with a wrangled moan. Wren cursed softly, but savagely. After another moment of holding me, Roane lifted his head to turn towards his brother. Lucan was unconscious.

"He's sleeping."

"Davy... what did you do?"

"His soul is intact."

Roane looked anguished. "He's human?"

I nodded.

"How?"

I couldn't tell him, not really. So I closed my eyes and when I opened them again, I let Roane see my true self. He saw the silver eyes. "I'm the Immortal."

To continue…

DAVY HARWOOD STILL IN TRANSITION

EPILOGUE

"Welcome to our last conversation."

I sighed in irritation and turned, but stopped in surprise. I looked around. "We're not in the dark anymore. And… I think I'm sleeping again."

The Immortal me stood before me. "No, we're not because this is the end."

I tilted my head questionably. "What are you talking about? I thought we were immortal, together for eternity?"

Silver eyes flashed back at me. "Stop thinking about trivial things. You don't need to distract yourself anymore."

"It's what I do." I shrugged it off, but something prickled at me. It was in the Immortal's voice—my voice. Then my eyes widened. It was *my* voice talking back to me. It wasn't the annoying Immortal or the lecturing Immortal. It was me.

Finally.

"What… what have I done again?"

The Immortal me smiled, assured and strong. "I did choose you, Davy, but I didn't go to you. When you reached inside of Talia, you pulled me out and inside of you. There's a part of you, a part that is noble. Your strength is more than I've ever encountered in a being before. You pulled me into you."

"That'd been my plan the whole time." My attempt at self-sarcasm was pathetic.

The other me continued, "There's a lot about being the Immortal that you don't understand. It's too much for you to know everything now, but things will be revealed as you go. You have a destiny and others will help you as you go. My part is done."

"What part was that?"

"My job was to help you accept who you are, who we are together. You accepted the Immortal, but you don't know the consequences. You will learn them as you go. I won't be the voice for those lessons."

I wasn't sure how I felt about this. What would I get instead?

"You've changed, Davy. You've become something new. This world is yours for the taking and you can make it better. There is a reason why the Immortal was created. You're not a fairytale. You're real and you are a force to be reckoned with. Do not let anyone take that from you. Do not!" She gutted out the last words, forcibly and urgent.

I had so many questions… so many new revelations… so many… so many of everything. I wanted to know it all, but then she said, "Welcome to your destiny. It is the beginning."

'Welcome to our last conversation.'

Then I woke up with a gasp. I was disoriented at first, feeling something warm around me. Then I heard cars honking in the distance. Slowly, I sat up and looked around. I was on the roof with a blanket draped over me. When I sat up, I smiled at the couch cushions that I'd been laying on.

"I brought you up here. Kates needed to sleep and I wanted some privacy. You both must've fallen asleep as soon as you got back to the room." Roane moved from the building's edge.

His eyes were still the same coal black, but there was something searching in them. He seemed softer, but he was dressed as such. Black pants with a crisp black shirt that wasn't tucked in. With his hardened jaw, he looked like ruthless—and he was.

His hand fell to his side and something flashed in the moonlight. It was his necklace.

I stood and gestured, half-heartedly. "You took that before. It's a leaf thing? What's it mean?"

He lifted it and stared at it long and hard. He murmured, "It was my brother's. I took it from him when I fought him. It was when Talia became the Immortal."

Oh. So much of that statement didn't sit comfortably with me. "I see…"

Roane took a deep breath and turned back to gaze over the city. The lights spread out for miles and as I moved beside him, the sight made me smile. Cars honked in the distance. People laughed. More lights flickered, but there was a stillness in the city.

I wasn't sure if it was Benshire or if it was me.

"I need to meet with the Roane Elders and give them this necklace."

"Why?" We'd just dealt with Lucan. I'd finally shown Roane that I was the Immortal. He was right when he said that Kates and I were tired. We both collapsed as soon as we got to the room. Everything had *just* happened…. I wasn't ready for him to leave me. Not yet.

"I have to tell them what happened. My brother is gone. After you left, some of his men took him. I have to tell them that my brother is human again and then I'm going to ask for the job of finding him. The necklace will be used to hunt him, for whoever is given the assignment."

Again…. Oh. I felt a sense of dread.

"Davy, things have happened that aren't understood."

Everything about that statement didn't bode well with anyone. I knew that things went smoother when they were understood. "How long do you think it'll take for you to find Lucan?"

How long was he going to be away?

"I don't know. It might take a few hours or months. He's human, but he still knows everything. He'll be dangerous. Lucan *liked* being a vampire. He'll want to become one again. I need to stop that from happening."

I nodded jerkily.

"They're not going to understand how you turned him human. That's not known by anyone and my Family were the ones entrusted to protect the Immortal. This is… this will not sit well with the Elders."

"Do you mean… am I in danger from them?"

From you?

"I don't know. When word gets out what you can do, you'll be feared by vampires. There aren't many who'd like to be human again. And you're Immortal. They can't kill you, which is what their first reaction will be. My Elders might want that too, but I'll argue on your behalf. I think they'll realize the foolishness of that."

I frowned as a different question formed in my head. "Roane, who is Jacith?"

His shoulders stiffened. "Where did you hear that name?"

"He was in Blue's head. The Immortal mentioned something about him."

Roane didn't like hearing any of that. "He's a *very* powerful witch, possibly the most powerful I've known."

"What does he have to do with the Immortal thread?"

Roane didn't answer right away, but eventually he did. "He created it."

Oh—whoa. I blinked in shock, but remembered the Immortal's words. Jacith thought he was powerful, but I was more. Somehow, I didn't think this Jacith would enjoy learning that information.

"Did he create the prophecy? Or just the Immortal thread?"

Roane had looked back over the city, but he whipped around once more to me. He had an accusing look in those dark eyes. "What are you talking about? Jacith created the Immortal. You talk as if the prophecy and the thread are separate. They are not. I assure you. My Family has volumes of Immortal lore. We were entrusted to protect the thread."

Except, they didn't know all of it and they didn't need to protect me. I knew about the separation from the Immortal. "You didn't know that I can turn vampires human."

Roane opened his mouth, but he couldn't argue my point. He closed it again as a look of mysticism crossed over his face.

I never thought I'd see that. I loved it.

"I thought I knew everything there was to know about Immortals. I'm starting to wonder if I know just a *little* about Immortals. It's unsettling."

"You don't understand, Roane. I... there's a prophecy that I think you don't know about. Someone created the prophecy and later someone else created the thread. I... I came to be before Jacith created the thread. I don't know why that's important, but it is. I know this because the Immortal told me. I told you before that we have conversations. She/it/me told me this... and someone else is going to guide me."

Roane turned and touched my shoulder. He turned me towards him. "Davy... the Immortal thread was created by Jacith. I know this, but... you're correct. He has never spoken about the ability for an Immortal to turn vampires into humans. If, in your conversations, you learn more then you must tell me. The Immortal is crucial to the vampire nation. We *must* know everything you know."

Something else didn't sit well with him. "What is it?"

Roane lifted up his head and gazed over the city's lights before he answered. "I was with Talia for years. I watched her grow and she never once talked about a conversation with the Immortal. It's so different. I... I don't know what to make of it. She would have odd dreams sometimes, but that was it."

I wasn't sure what stung me more: Talia and Roane or the lack of conversations. I could've done without those conversations. "I'm the last, Roane. The Immortal told me. I'm the last to be the Immortal. I'm not a carrier for the thread. I *am* the Immortal."

'Do not let anyone take that from you.'

Roane was silent.

I continued, "It's just the beginning, Roane. I know that your next step is finding your brother, but it's just the beginning for me. There's so much more. I can feel it. I know it."

Roane looked at me gravely. He stared long and hard. He didn't try to slip inside. I didn't try to slip inside of him. We remained in our own bodies. No powers. No thought reading.

"Are you looking for my soul?"

Slowly, he shook his head and took my hand. His fingers slid against mine and locked in place. I closed my eyes and savored the feeling. Strength radiated off of him, perhaps for what was to come.

Then he whispered, "I'm looking for mine."

WWW.TIJANSBOOKS.COM

CPSIA information can be obtained
at www.ICGtesting.com
Printed in the USA
LVHW081656270422
717391LV00011B/536

9 781951 771195